Tempting the Deputy

Tempting the Deputy

A Men of Marietta Romance

Heidi Rice

TULE
PUBLISHING

Tempting the Deputy
Copyright © 2017 Heidi Rice
Tule Publishing First Printing, April 2017

The Tule Publishing Group, LLC

ISBN: 978-1-946772-36-7

Chapter One

THE STRETCH OF I-89 winding down the mountain pass into Marietta was one of the prettiest stretches of highway in the whole of Montana. Hell, the whole of the USA. With Yellowstone fifty-four miles to the south and Bozeman twenty-four miles to the north, the two-lane road crossed over the Marietta River and had the towering snow-capped peak of Copper Mountain staring down on it like a slumbering giant in hues of purple and gray as the sun sunk toward the horizon.

Logan Tate hated every damn inch of it.

But especially the inches that snaked through Copper Canyon, and then hit the lowland, as the Douglas firs gave way to Ponderosa pines and grasslands.

His hands tensed on the steering wheel of his squad car as he came round the bend in the road near where Harry Monroe had died one dark, rainy night during Labor Day weekend while changing a tire for an elderly couple on the roadside.

He steeled himself against the flood of memories.

"Go on, Logan. You look beat. I've got this. I can change a

damn tire without help, buddy."

And the flood of guilt that followed.

Nothing good had ever come of driving down this damn road, for Logan. He could still remember another dark, rainy night when he'd been squished in between his daddy and his baby brother Lyle in the front seat of the family's beat-up old pickup truck. The moment when the lights of the ambulance just ahead of them had stopped flashing—and his daddy had started cussing, with tears leaking out of his eyes.

Lyle had started bawling because he was scared and tired and only four years old. And Logan had been left frozen, terrified to cry in case it made his daddy even madder. He'd never heard his daddy swear before, let alone cuss God like that. Logan knew his mommy would be mad to hear his daddy talk that way. But he didn't want to think about his mommy. Or why his daddy had gotten him and Lyle out of bed in the middle of the night. Or how his mommy had looked so pale and still as the men in navy pants and button-up shirts had carried her into the ambulance.

Sometimes he felt as if he'd been frozen ever since.

Logan pressed his foot on the gas, allowing his speed to creep up to just below the legal limit after clearing the bend in the highway. He rubbed the scar on his chest beneath his deputy's badge. Funny to think he'd once been shocked to hear his father cuss.

The sun was lowering now over the ridge, but it was a good two hours before night would fall. He needed to get back to Marietta, report to the Sheriff and then clock off his shift as a reserve Sheriff's Deputy, before heading back to the ranch to feed the cows they'd already moved into the calving field, then make it to Grey's by eight. Lyle better damn well be there tonight—Marietta's First Responders had an important meeting about what to do with the shortfall in the funding for Harry's House. The house they were rehabbing on Church Avenue to honor their friend's memory, which would house teenagers and troubled kids who needed a place to feel safe.

He hadn't seen Lyle in four days, after his smoke-jumping brother had been called up out of fire season to assist at an emergency over in Gallatin County. But Logan had gotten word from one of the First Responders in Bozeman the smoke jumpers had been called off the job over ten hours ago. So where the hell was Lyle? Because he hadn't bothered to call and let his brother know he was okay. Probably busy working off the adrenaline rush in some bar in Livingston. As soon as he saw Lyle, he was going to give his kid brother a hug to make sure he was still whole, still solid—and then he was going to give him hell.

As he drove past the exact spot Harry had died, Logan's eye caught sight of something—or someone—crouching on the edge of a clump of Ponderosa pines thirty yards away. He eased his foot off the gas and braked.

Parking the car on the shoulder, he searched the roadside for a vehicle but couldn't see one in either direction.

He pulled his weapon out of the glove compartment and stepped out of the car, securing the weapon in the holster on his belt as per regulation. Then he fished out the binoculars to be sure what he thought he'd seen was actually real, and not a figment of his sometimes too vivid imagination. But as he focused in on a heart-stopping face he didn't recognize, short unruly hair, and slender limbs dressed in jeans and boots and a checkered shirt, his heart skipped a couple of beats.

And then annoyance kicked in.

What the hell? Where had that girl come from? And what the hell was she doing ten miles from town without any means of transportation? Night was coming in fast and when it did, the temperature would drop like a stone. They'd had an unseasonably warm spell in the last couple of weeks, which had melted all the snow in the lowlands, but the nights could still be brutal.

She had to be a tourist. Nobody from Marietta would be dumb enough to get stranded out here without a vehicle. He watched her for a moment.

Yup, definitely a damn tourist.

She was taking pictures. Who knew what of, out here in the middle of nowhere.

Well, she wouldn't be taking them for too much longer.

He stuffed the binoculars back in the glove compartment. Then radioed it in.

"Hey, Betty. I'm gonna be late in off shift."

"Is there a problem, Logan? Anything I need tell Sheriff Walton about?" Betty, the Sheriff's Office dispatcher patched back.

"Just a lost tourist out on I-89. I'll handle it."

"A lost tourist? On I-89? *Where* on I-89?" Betty said, because as well as being a top-level dispatcher she was also a top-level gossip.

"Quarter mile past the bend out of Copper Canyon. There's no sign of a vehicle, so I'll offer her a ride into town." A ride he would make damn sure she accepted. No one else was going to die out here on his watch. Not if he could help it.

"Her? So it's a lady?" Betty asked, her interest clearly piqued.

"Uh-huh, gotta go. Over and out," Logan barked and hung up the radio, before he could get drawn into an in-depth discussion that would get broadcast all over town before nightfall.

After pulling his shearling jacket out of the car, because there was already a substantial chill in the air, that the girl seemed to be unaware of, he shrugged the jacket on and began the trek toward her, determined to keep his face impassive, and his temper in check.

That the girl didn't have the sense God gave a gopher was obvious. That she'd chosen the wrong place and the wrong time to get lost even more so, because Deputy Logan Tate was so not in the mood to rescue pretty tourists today.

✪

CHARLOTTE FOSTER ADJUSTED the f-stop on her Leica and fired off another ten shots of the mountain. The pine boughs framing the shots added a splash of vibrant green to the deep turquoise blue of the sky, the stark juniper green of the wintry pasture, and the mulberry wine glow of the rocky edifice in the background. Standing up, she checked her viewfinder and felt her heartbeat slow and her breath squeeze in her lungs. A sure sign she'd taken a perfect shot.

She squinted back up at the mountain. The light was glorious here. She'd never encountered anything quite like it. And they were still at least forty minutes from magic hour: that enchanted sixty minutes just before full dark fell when the natural landscape became suffused in a golden glow.

She rubbed her arms, and then breathed into her fingers, noticing the dropping temperature for the first time. Screwing her camera back onto its tripod, she reached into her pack and rummaged around for a sweater and her fingerless gloves. The cold didn't scare her, the exhilarating thought of all the amazing pictures she was going to take more than enough to stave off the threat of frostbite.

"Hey there, Miss."

Charlotte's head shot up, and for the first time she noticed the man approaching her from the road, his tall, broad frame cast into shadow by the sinking sun. Panic kicked in for a nanosecond and she touched the can of mace she kept in her pack, until she spotted the squad car behind him and the badge pinned to his shirt. She dropped the mace and straightened. He had to be some kind of law enforcement officer despite the battered jeans and boots and thick leather jacket with a sheep fur collar. Which was good on one level—he was unlikely to be a serial killer. Not so good on another. Charlie had never been great with authority figures.

"Hi," she said, shrugging on her sweater. Was she trespassing? She hadn't even thought to ask the bus driver who'd finally agreed to drop her off here. She'd been way too busy concocting a story about the mythical rancher boyfriend who was due to pick her up and was running a bit late.

Men in Montana took the whole weaker sex thing way too seriously for her liking.

"Can I ask what you're doing out here, Miss?"

He stepped out of the shadow and into the light, and Charlie's breath seized. Just like it had when she'd checked her viewfinder a few moments before. Like the rugged scenery, the man's face was beautiful in a rough-hewn way. The granite-hard jaw, dark brows, broken nose, and strikingly blue eyes complemented by the most sensual pair of lips she had ever seen. Full and bowed and surrounded by the shadow of stubble, they should have looked girly but didn't. Every molecule of saliva in her mouth dried up, her heart pounding so hard in her chest she felt a bit light-headed.

"Miss?" he murmured.

She jerked her gaze away from those tantalizing lips. And

saw knowledge and intensity and the hint of frustration in his eyes, which she suddenly realized were as deep and pure a blue as the Montana sky. And two things occurred to her at once.

I want to photograph you—and jump you, too.

"Nothing illegal," she said, suddenly feeling besieged.

The badge on his chest—his very impressive chest—glinted in the dying sunlight. What a shame Deputy Sexy Lips was a lawman. Charlie's natural instinct to rebel against any kind of constraint had got her into no end of trouble as a teenager, when she'd been expelled from every fancy boarding school in the UK her parents had sent her to. And some of the unfancy ones, too.

Down, girl, you do not want to jump him. He'd be way too much work—and probably boring in bed. The type who always insisted on being on top.

But her fingers still itched to pick up her camera. That face. She definitely wanted to photograph that face. She did a quick once-over of his impressive build. And she could just imagine what an amazing body he would have. She would definitely love to photograph that body too, preferably *sans* clothing. And *sans* badge.

"Then it won't be a problem telling me what it is you were doing?" he said, in that I'm-the-boss-of-you tone that should have been pissing her off. But was turning her on a little bit. Annoyingly.

"Right, no. I'm just…" *For God's sake, Charlie, stop acting like an escaped convict.* "Taking some shots of your mountain. The light here's incredible."

He tipped his head to glance up at the mountain, almost as if he'd forgotten it was there, then cast that penetrating gaze back on her. "That's as may be," he said, as if he doubted it. "But it'll be dark in an hour or so, and I can't let you stay out here on your own."

I can't let you?

Okay, forget those kissable lips—that was not going to endear him to her. "As long as I'm not breaking any laws, Officer…?" She waited politely for him to fill in his name.

"Deputy Logan Tate," he said.

"Deputy Logan Tate," she said, going the full obsequious. "I'm fairly sure that's not your decision. It's mine."

"That's where you're wrong, Miss…?" He waited in turn. Forcing her to give up her name, too.

"Charlotte Foster." Not that anyone ever called her Charlotte. All her friends called her Charlie, but somehow she did not think she and Deputy Sexy Lips were ever going to be friends.

"Miss Charlotte Foster," he said, sounding the opposite of obsequious. "Once the sun goes down out here, the temperature will drop to below freezing. I don't see a vehicle anywhere—so I'm giving you a ride into town, where you can get a warm bed for the night." His eyes narrowed, daring her to contradict him. Unfortunately even she couldn't make up a car that clearly did not exist. And somehow she didn't think her mythical boyfriend would stand up to that laconic scrutiny either—which left her with only one option. Get snotty back.

"Really, that won't be necessary," she said, smiling through gritted teeth. "I can always hitch into town when I'm ready."

"Hitch?" His eyebrows shot up, as if she'd just said she was planning to sprout wings and fly into town. "I can't let you do that either. It's not safe."

There he went with the not-letting-her-do-stuff thing again. Her back muscles locked as her spine stiffened.

She didn't think mentioning she'd hitched a couple of times already with no ill effects, or telling him about her trusty mace, was going to wipe the judgmental frown off his face, so she changed tack.

"If you don't think hitching is safe in this area, I'd be foolish not to take your advice, Deputy." She resisted the urge to bat her eyelashes at him. Somehow she didn't think he was the type to appreciate sarcasm. "But not to worry, I've got a tent and a sleeping bag." She indicated her pack. "I can always camp out."

She noticed the ticking muscle in his jaw, but his gaze didn't falter. "From your accent, I'm guessing you're not from around here."

"I'm British, originally, but I've been touring the US for the last six months and I've lived in Manhattan for a number of years." And she was a professional photographer with exhibitions in London, New York, and Paris and several prestigious awards under her belt, not to mention a contract to do a coffee table book on America's Hidden Heartlands and regular commissions with *Vanity Fair*, *Vogue*, and a long list of other glossy magazines. But she decided not to mention any of that. Somehow she didn't think Deputy Sexy Lips was a *Vanity Fair* subscriber.

"But have you ever camped out around here?"

"Well, no I've never…"

"Because no one in their right mind would camp out here in March."

Charlie tucked her hands into the back pockets of her jeans and tried to get a firm grip of her temper. "I have a fifty-tog sleeping bag that can withstand a night on Everest," she said in her reasonable voice. "I will be fine."

"I don't care if you've got a five-hundred tog sleeping bag that can withstand a month in the North Pole. I'm not leaving you out here tonight. So why don't you gather up your stuff and we can get going."

The Deputy Formerly Known as Sexy Lips, who she'd just rechristened Deputy Hard-Ass flicked his eyes down for a moment. Heat arched between them. Had he just checked out her breasts? The ticking muscle in his jaw went as hard as the granite mountain she'd spent the afternoon admiring.

"You can't make me go," she said, her temper slipping through her numbing fingers. But at that precise moment a gush of frigid wind whistled over the pasturelands and right through her sweater. Her teeth chattered as a shiver wracked her body.

He swore softly under his breath. And she knew, from the dangerous look in his eyes, that there was no way on earth he was going to let her stay here for the hour she needed to get her perfect shot. She wanted to swear, too. A lot. The thought of losing the shot because of Deputy Hard-Ass's Neanderthal attitude to women made her want to scream.

"Yeah, I can," he said, his voice as deep as it was firm. "You've got a choice. You can either get in that squad car without an argument. Or I can cuff you, and arrest you and put you in it. Either way you'll be riding into town now. But one way you get to ride up front, the other you ride in the back and get to spend a night in the cells."

"You can't arrest me? What for?"

"For jaywalking," he said.

"But I'm not jaywalking," she said. Not that she was exactly sure what jaywalking was.

"Walking down a highway would qualify."

"But I'm not on the highway. And since when is walking down a road an arrestable offence?" If they arrested people for that in Manhattan they'd have to lock up the whole city.

"It is, if I say it is," he said, the tiny twitch on those wide sexy lips antagonizing her more.

Was he finding this amusing? Because she sure as hell wasn't. She wanted to stay out here and take her shots. This was her professional career. But more than that, she could feel the shimmer of excitement in her blood, always triggered when she knew she was on the cusp of taking an amazing shot. And it could only be the prospect of that causing it this time, too… Because her weird reaction to him was becoming less and less explainable the more snotty he became. Getting pushed around was not high on her list of turn-ons. Even by guys who looked like he did.

"If you're going to arrest me, go ahead." *Sod obsequious.* "But I'm not leaving until you do."

She turned her back on him, which was her second mistake. The tiny jingle of metal on metal was followed by the cold touch of steel and the soft click on her wrist. She spun round, shocked into silence, when he took her other wrist in firm callused hands and snapped the other handcuff shut.

"I'm arresting you for jaywalking on I-89, Miss Charlotte Foster."

"You have got to be kidding me?" she managed, the surge of something that made no sense at all annoying her almost as much as the shock of getting handcuffed.

Instead of answering, he stared her down with those cool blue eyes, and began reciting a load of rights at her, which he reeled off in a deadly serious monotone. But she could see that slight twitch on his lips was still there.

Good grief, he is totally getting off on this.

She wanted to be outraged; unfortunately she couldn't quite be, because she could feel the melting sensation in her abdomen as he lifted her pack and her tripod on to one shoulder as if they weighed nothing at all.

"Come on," he said, grasping her arm above the elbow and leading her to the squad car. "The sooner we get you into town, the sooner I can charge you and throw you in a nice warm cell for the night."

"You're actually serious? You're going to imprison me for being sixty feet from a road?" She was so completely astonished by the turn of events—the cold steel of the handcuffs clamped on her wrists and the warm feel of his fingers firm on her arm as he directed her to the car—that she was still struggling to get to her outrage.

She'd met hard-asses before. She had never met anyone as hard-assed as this guy.

He opened the back door of the car, dumped her pack and her camera inside, and then placed his other hand on her head to direct her into the seat. After buckling her into the car, he slammed the door and got into the driver's seat in front, then spoke through the grill.

"You'll thank me for it, Charlotte, when you're warm and cozy in a cell tonight and not dying of hypothermia." The twitch gave way and a lopsided smile tipped up those beautiful lips.

Heat suffused her cheeks, and concentrated at her core.

Damn the man for being even more sexy when he was patronizing her.

She sent him an angry glare, and then ignored him, finally locating her outrage.

"I very much doubt that," she grumbled under her breath as the rich redolent glow of happy hour began to roll across the landscape.

The car pulled onto the road and she watched her perfect shot disappear out the back window.

It took twenty minutes to drive into the nearby town. Charlie fumed every second of the way in the back seat. Cursing Deputy Hard-Ass, America's ludicrous highway code, and her big mouth but most of all her sex-starved libido, which—if the liquid warmth in her abdomen was anything to go by—had so lost the plot it had decided that getting manhandled by a guy who obviously enjoyed bossing women about was actually sort of hot.

★

CONSTERNATION HAD GIVEN way to panic and dismay as the squad car passed the high-wire fences of a school football field. Charlie glared at the back of her tormentor's head.

Why had she taken him on? Why had she talked back to him and practically dared him to arrest her? An arrest could jeopardize her green card. She'd been living in the States for five years now and was already a feature on the New York art scene. Her shows had gotten write-ups in the press and she'd really broken through last year with an award-winning spread in *National Geographic*.

This book was her chance to finally hit the mainstream—but not if she had to return to the UK with a slap on the wrist from the Department of Immigration. And even worse than that, what would her sister Emily do if she heard? That would be the biggest catastrophe of all.

Em was precisely two minutes older than her, but had declared herself the big sister and had acted accordingly ever since they were toddlers. Where Charlie was reckless and spontaneous, Em was responsible and frankly way too uptight. She'd probably come swooping down to read Deputy Hard-Ass the riot act for abuse of power or some such nonsense. The way she had when they were sixteen years old, and Charlie had gotten caught smoking weed and snogging Jack Murray in the gym after lights out.

Em had been magnificent that day, defending Charlie to the stuffy headmaster Mr. Carmichael with a passion and purpose that Charlie knew she did not deserve—because, of course, Charlie had been guilty as sin. Consequently they'd ended up both getting expelled. Charlie for breaking two fairly major school rules pertaining to drugs and boys and Em, the model student, for insubordination. Em being Em she'd never even given Charlie a guilt trip for bringing another perfect school record to an ignominious end, but Charlie had felt lower than dirt nonetheless.

After managing to survive for the last six years—ever since she'd turned eighteen and used the money their parents had left them to travel the globe and make her dream of becoming a photographer a reality—without getting any more black marks against her permanent record, she did not want to freak Em out with this news.

All of which meant she was going to have to figure out a way to hold on to her temper—not to mention the inappropriate urge to jump Deputy Hard-Ass—when they arrived at the Sheriff's Office. And schmooze the pants off the bastard.

Unfortunately there wasn't much Charlie found harder than having to control her natural urges. So she needed to come up with a strategy. Em had always sworn by being properly prepared for any unforeseen disasters—getting unexpectedly arrested on a highway in Montana would definitely qualify.

Detaching her gaze from the back of the lawman's neck, she tried to rack her brain to think about what she should do to persuade Deputy Hard-Ass he was way out of line, without pissing him off more in the process, but then she noticed the elegant wooden sign announcing the entrance to Old Town Marietta.

Her breath clogged as the cruiser turned onto the town's Main Street and she took in the wood-framed buildings. She'd read a little bit about the town in her research for her trip. The place had been built in the late 1800s on the proceeds from the copper found in the aptly named Copper Mountain. But she hadn't expected anything quite so stunning, its history preserved so beautifully. Her fingers itched to grab her camera.

Main Street stretched up toward what looked like a park

and a magnificent nineteenth-century courthouse building, the majestic peaks of the surrounding mountains framing the scene like something out of a western movie. It was a dream location for any photographer. The dynamic juxtaposition of man and nature, old and new, functional and fanciful captured Charlie's imagination—she could spend a lifetime photographing this place.

She swiveled her head, trying to keep the scene in view as the car drifted past an ornate Catholic church and then turned a corner on to a side street. The car took another turn and pulled to a stop in front of a glass-fronted utilitarian building between the back of the church and a firehouse, the Sheriff's Department logo etched onto the front window— next to that of the Police Department. Charlie's heartbeat ticked back into her throat, and threatened to choke her.

Bugger. She was supposed to have been coming up with a strategy to charm a guy with about as much give in him as a lump of granite from that mountain, not getting captivated by the town's old-world charm.

Her tormentor got out of the driver's seat and opened her door. "Up you get," he said, reaching in to take her arm and help her out of the car.

She stepped onto the sidewalk, steadfastly ignoring the prickle of sensation snaking its way up her arm from the firm pressure of his fingers. The guy had the whole take-charge thing down pat.

She stood shivering from reaction more than the cold as

he reached in to grab her pack.

Say something, you silly moo. The charm offensive starts now.

"Listen, Deputy Hard-Ass..." *Crap. Don't call him that.* "I mean Deputy..." She glanced at the name badge pinned to his shirt as he straightened to his full height and deposited her pack and her camera tripod on the sidewalk—his expression disconcertingly inscrutable. She had to tip her head back to see his face.

How tall was he? At least six-three, for goodness' sake.

"Deputy Tate," she corrected herself. "Really there's no need to arrest me. I have absolutely learnt my lesson." Next time she'd make sure she kept an eye out for marauding do-gooders while she was taking her pictures.

"And what lesson is that?" he said, in that rumble of sound that seemed to come up from deep inside his chest. His very broad, very magnificent chest.

Stop looking at his chest. Focus, Charlie, focus. Or your American adventure is going to come to an abrupt end.

Her gaze jerked to his face, but the arresting combination of tough-as-granite jaw, sky-blue eyes and far-too-kissable lips dazzled her for a moment.

"Um..." What had they been talking about?

"You'll have to be more specific," he said.

Her temper prickled, seeing the glint of amusement. She searched her mind for something to say that would appease him, while ignoring the muscle twitching in his cheek that was having an unpredictable effect on her libido.

"I've learned that lawmen in Montana take the whole serve and protect thing very seriously," she managed at last.

One skeptical eyebrow lifted, and the muscle kept twitching. Obviously one not-entirely-sincere compliment wasn't going to be enough to satisfy his I'm-the-boss-of-you complex. Maybe a shot to his common sense would do the trick.

She lifted her hands, making the cuffs jangle.

"Come on, Deputy, uncuff me. You're not really going to arrest me for taking a few photographs. That's just silly. Imagine if the story got out? It would be a disaster for the Marietta tourist trade." A town that looked as breathtaking as this one must do a roaring tourist trade. "Surely you of all people wouldn't want to jeopardize that?"

The skeptical eyebrow lowered and she realized she'd made a major tactical error. However much of a hard-ass Deputy Hard-Ass was, he wasn't stupid. Because he'd understood exactly what she had implied—that tourists like her paid his salary.

"A tourist freezing to death out on the highway would be worse for the tourist trade."

The laconic tone made it clear she was the one being patronized.

"I don't know what you expect me to say?" she said, refusing to take the only other option open to her.

She didn't care how much trouble it would get her in with the authorities… And her twin sister… The one thing she was not prepared to do was beg.

She'd done that once before, with her parents. The night before she and Em had been sent off to their first boarding school. And all it had done was make her feel small and insignificant. She'd promised herself after she'd cried herself to sleep that night she would never beg anyone for anything again. Much better to simply seal off your emotions, then you would never ever have to hurt that way again.

Not that Deputy Hard-Ass had the power to hurt her, no man did. Because she never got that invested in relationships. But his take-charge attitude and killer face and physique had already had an unpredictable effect on her libido. So cutting this conversation off at the pass would be a smart move.

"I expect you to say you'll stay safe from now on," he said. "And not do dumb things like hitch rides with strangers or camp out in below-freezing temperatures."

Her heartbeat punched her ribs, the simple, stupidly overprotective statement touching the raw nerve she thought she'd cut out a lifetime ago.

"Well I'm not saying that," she shot back. "Because the risks I decide to take with my personal safety are none of your business."

✪

LOGAN STARED AT the girl—her short hair rioting around that slender face made her look like an enraged pixie—and tried to tramp down on the twin tides of admiration and arousal.

Jesus, she was quite the little firecracker.

Who the hell got riled about being given a ride into town so they wouldn't freeze their butt off in the middle of a forest?

His intention had never been to actually arrest her, only to teach her a lesson about personal responsibility. And yeah, paying attention to her own personal safety dammit. And he refused to feel bad about that.

But now he had a problem on his hands. Because he could all but feel Betty's eyes boring holes into the back of his skull as she watched this exchange from the station house's front desk. And he didn't have a damn thing to actually charge Charlotte Foster with. Cuffing her had been over the top enough, but it was the only way he could see to get her into the damn car before they both froze their butts off.

Something about the way she had squared off to him and challenged him and insisted on putting herself in danger had called on all his natural instincts to serve and protect and some unnatural ones that he did not intend to examine too closely.

If he thought he'd seen a similar spark of arousal in her eyes he was not going to dwell on that either. He liked his sex life predictable—that way it didn't get in the way of the rest of his life. And this spark of arousal, the desire to cuff her and then sink his fingers into that wild hair and hold her in place so he could ravish those sweet cherry red lips until she moaned her surrender against his mouth wasn't predictable. Hell, it probably wasn't even legal. So there was no way on earth he would ever act on it.

But after arguing with her for ten minutes out front of the Station House, the urge to pick her up and fling her over his shoulder and carry her off somewhere dark and private where he could show her exactly who was boss was starting to get the better of him again. And that could not be good. Because Logan Tate didn't have unpredictable, unnatural urges. And even if he did, he sure as hell didn't act on them.

But even as the smart, sensible, steadfast part of him was telling him to defuse the situation, something else entirely came out of his mouth.

"It sure as hell *is* my business, when you're planning to put yourself at risk of frostbite or worse in my town."

Her eyes flashed green fire, and her chin jutted out as if she were planning to challenge him to hand-to-hand combat and he felt the tug of reaction deep in his crotch.

Damn, he'd never found feisty women a turn-on. But there was a sense of vulnerability beneath that tough outer shell that called to his inner caveman.

"Go ahead and charge me then, Deputy Hard-Ass," she said, squaring off to him.

I don't want to arrest you. I want to spank you and then make love to you until we both can't walk straight.

The erotic thought came so far out of left field, it was like a bucket of ice-cold water thrown over him.

He stepped back.

He would never raise a hand to any woman. They were the fairer sex. There to be respected and treated with care and attention at all costs. He'd never even had rough sex before—the urge quashed before it could take root—but he'd cuffed and, yeah, manhandled this woman without due cause.

And gotten pretty damn close to taking things a whole lot further.

He pulled the key for the cuffs out of the pocket of his jeans. "I'm not going to charge you this time," he said, undoing the cuffs—and clipping them back onto his belt. He saw her shoulders sag with relief, and felt like the worse kind of bully.

No better than his father.

Shame engulfed him as he noticed the slight redness on the delicate skin of her wrist. Without thinking, he took her hand and massaged the pale flesh with gentle fingers, the way he would stroke the newborn baby calves.

"You should have told me they were hurting," he said.

"I didn't notice." She trembled and their eyes connected. What he saw shocked him to his core. Damn, she was as turned on as he was. What the heck was happening here?

He could feel the rapid beat of her pulse beneath his thumb and arousal surged. He could feel himself getting hard. He needed to get away from this girl. She was bad for him. But even as he acknowledged the need to keep his distance from her and the powerful effect she had on him, his thumb pressed against the delicate flutter of her pulse and the thought of that little flash of vulnerability he'd spotted beneath the feisty façade had him adding: "You can go, as long as I get your word you won't do anything dumb—like hitching out of town tonight."

She stiffened and drew her hands out of his. For a moment he thought he'd blown it and she was going to refuse. And then he'd be forced to charge her. Because no way in hell was he risking her going back out on to the highway again tonight. But then her lips tipped up on one side. And her green eyes sparkled with mischief.

Which only made her more damn attractive.

"My word?" she said, as if testing the request for flaws.

"Yeah, your word of honor."

She grinned outright then, the smile so smug it was as infuriating as it was spellbinding. He had the perverse thought that if that was how she looked when she was sexually satisfied he could get a real kick out of holding her right on the edge of orgasm for hours.

Not appropriate, Tate. Not appropriate at all.

"Absolutely you can have my word of honor," she said, the knowing light in her eyes telling him loud and clear she considered the whole concept of honor and accountability as outdated and inconsequential as following the rules he'd spent his whole life living by.

She lifted her pack onto one slender shoulder. He resisted the urge to offer to help her as she picked up the camera tripod.

"I'll see you around, Deputy," she said, rolling the address off her tongue, reminding him of the nickname that had slipped out during their argument.

Deputy Hard-Ass.

Instead of calling her on the cheeky comment, he tapped two fingers to his forehead in a mock salute.

As she walked off toward Our Lady of the Angels Catholic Church on the corner of 4th and Front Avenue, he noticed the sway of her slender hips in the tomboy jeans and the shot of heat hit him squarely in the crotch.

"Not if I see you first," he murmured beneath his breath as he slammed the squad car door and tore his eyes away from her butt.

Charlotte Foster was trouble.

Smart-mouthed, feisty, and far too sexy trouble. Exactly the sort of trouble he did not need in his life. Because he had enough trouble already dealing with the upcoming calving season, his kid brother Lyle's addiction to jumping out of planes into the middle of forest infernos, and figuring out how he and the rest of Marietta's First Responders were going to raise enough money to bring Harry's House up to code in less than ninety days.

The good news was, Miss Foster was a tourist who would

be gone on the first bus out of town tomorrow morning.

Not so good was the squeeze of regret as he watched her slim figure stroll round the back of the church and disappear.

Chapter Two

*F*OR SUCH A *small town, Marietta, Montana, certainly has way more than its fair share of prime man candy.*

Charlie nursed her second bottle of beer and enjoyed the impromptu floor show in Grey's Saloon supplied by the group of guys standing ten feet away having a heated discussion about some place called Harry's House.

All of them topped six foot and every single one of them had shoulders wide enough and butts tight enough and faces ruggedly handsome enough to leave any woman breathless. Especially a woman who hadn't gotten laid since last September—and she wasn't sure the one-night stand she'd had with the curator after the preview of her last New York showing even counted. The celebratory encounter in his penthouse had been the sexual equivalent of watching wood warp, very slowly.

Surely her sex drought had to explain her bizarre reaction to Deputy Hard-Ass a couple of hours ago too—which she was totally over now, because she was already appreciating the prime assets of other men. Ten other men to be precise.

So what if this smorgasbord of earthly delights wasn't

giving her quite the same buzz that her bossy arresting officer had earlier in the evening. She took another sip of the icy local brew and savored the sight laid out before her, determined to get turned on if it killed her.

The men's body language was certainly making the shadowy booth of the local saloon feel pleasantly warm, the discussion obviously something they were all passionate about.

"We can't risk losing the house. That'd set the project back for months, maybe even years," the guy in a dark green uniform shirt said. Charlie had christened him Forest Ranger Hottie. She'd noticed he had a sort of world-weariness about him, a guardedness that made him not quite part of the group. She'd seen the same kind of behavior in guys she'd photographed coming back from service in Iraq. Guys who had seen too much.

She coughed out a laugh at the romanticism of her thoughts. How he'd managed to get so guarded as a Forest Ranger she had no idea given the breathtaking beauty of the local countryside. Perhaps forest management could be more stressful than she thought.

"Which is why we have to come up with a plan to raise the money, like yesterday," the guy she'd dubbed Fireman Hottie chipped in. Charlie couldn't quite shake the thought that he looked vaguely familiar, the classically handsome bone structure and the magnetic dimple in his chin definitely reminding her of someone even though she knew she'd never met him before.

"So we step up to the plate as Marietta's First Responders and make damn sure it gets done," said the only other guy in uniform apart from Forest Ranger Hottie, the vibrant red jacket he'd discarded on entering the saloon setting him apart as Search and Rescue Hottie.

The other guys all nodded or spoke their agreement.

"Where are Logan and Lyle?" Fireman Hottie added. "It was their idea for us to come up with a fundraising plan. I thought they'd be here by now."

Logan? Not...

Charlie hadn't even had the chance to finish the thought when her worst nightmare swung open the saloon doors and marched into the bar.

All the oxygen sucked out of the room as Charlie slid further back into the shadows of her booth. She took a long gulp of her beer, but it failed to chill the geyser of heat working its way up her torso at the sight of him.

He'd lost the badge and the gun belt, but none of the attitude as he strode up to the long wooden bar to be greeted by his friends. She watched him unobserved, the pleasant buzz from checking out the other hotties becoming a firework display worthy of London's new year celebrations on the Thames.

Crapola. Even with all this prime man candy on display, only Deputy Hard-Ass had the power to make her go up in flames.

What on earth was that about? Had the Montana air turned her into a masochist? Or a nymphomaniac? Because until this evening, she would have said she was not the sort of girl who got off on being bossed about.

He didn't spot her, his attention focused on the other First Responder dudes as they greeted him. The discussion continued as they suggested and discarded ways to make money for their pet project. Charlie was only listening with half an ear now, though—all her attention pinned on the man whose superpower was to totally mess with her karma. Then another guy entered the bar, swelling the hotness smorgasbord to a round dozen.

This guy was leaner than Logan and nowhere near as moody, his dark blond hair contrasting with Deputy Hard-Ass's darker coloring to make him light to Logan's shade. As soon as he arrived, the new hottie energized the group with his wide grin and backslapping bonhomie. Everyone except Deputy Hard-Ass, who gripped the new guy's shoulders, gave him a man hug, then glared at him.

The tension radiating from his big, buff body made the fireworks in Charlie's core go a little berserk, but everyone else seemed to be oblivious to his brooding, the new guy most of all, who ignored the frown of disapproval as his other friends all made a fuss of him. The name Lyle got bandied about as they congratulated him on his heroics during an emergency incident in a neighboring county.

Well, hello, Smoke Jumper Hottie.

No wonder these guys were all so buff, obviously First Responder was a euphemism for local hero. They spent their time rescuing the local populace. Well, all except Deputy Hard-Ass, who spent his time arresting innocent jaywalkers.

Charlie finished off her drink and decided she'd hidden in the shadowy booth long enough. She'd never been the sort of woman to back down from a challenge. And Deputy Hard-Ass was certainly that.

She'd let him get the upper hand during their earlier showdown.

When she'd given him her word that she wouldn't leave town, she'd planned to break it as soon as she walked past the church. But somehow she hadn't quite been able to hitch straight back out onto the highway—eventually ending up at a picture-perfect Bed and Breakfast on the outskirts of town run by a woman who looked like an angel, but appeared to have the work ethic of a Trojan.

She'd taken a load of shots of the town on her walk to the bar this evening, all of which would make great fodder for her blog on America's hidden heartlands—and had made the decision to stay for a while longer, maybe even a couple of weeks to get more shots of the town. She could already tell Marietta was rich with opportunities to document an essential part of small-town life in the US for her book project.

But if she was going to stay, she needed to make it crystal clear to Logan Tate that he could not interfere with her plans—which meant getting all up in his face, thus showing him that no one bossed Charlie Foster about. Not even men with buns of steel and quite possibly the most kissable lips on the planet.

She wound her way back toward the long wooden bar, sensing the exact moment when Logan Tate spotted her. The small hairs on the back of her neck stood to attention and she turned to find his striking sky-blue eyes locked on hers. The intense stare burned right through her clothing, making every inch of skin feel exposed. She stared right back, her heart leaping along with the surge of pheromones doing a happy dance as she imagined framing that hot, heated look in the viewfinder of her Leica.

At that precise moment a blast of divine inspiration came from on high—or more likely from way down below in the lower reaches of hell—and struck her right in her solar plexus.

Oh. My. God. I have the perfect solution to their fundraising problem.

A solution that could also solve her issues with Deputy Hard-Ass—and put him right where she wanted him, at her beck and call in front of her camera lens.

Giving in to the urge to jump the guy was not going to happen. She did not do complex relationships. And this guy—and her unexplainable reaction to him—had complication written all over it. But leaving town now without getting to photograph him was not going to happen. She had killer instincts about her photography, and this guy could be the cover shot for her book.

The essence of American manhood. Tough, taciturn, and take-charge—with a hottie quotient that was off the charts. But asking him politely to sit for her after their earlier run-in was out of the question—not only might it require her to beg, but she was also fairly sure the guy would say no just to be pissy—so she was going to have to get sneaky.

And as luck would have it, Marietta's First Responders and their charity project had just provided her with the perfect opportunity to make sure Deputy Hard-Ass would have to pose for her, preferably with as few clothes as possible—if she could persuade his friends to go for the idea. And she knew she could.

She'd done a commission last year in Chicago for a fire-house that had wanted to raise money to help the widow and children of one of their own who had been lost in a house fire in Lincoln Park. They'd contacted her through her website—after a *National Geographic* shoot she did on Pennsylvania steelworkers had gotten a lot of attention—and she'd been happy to waive her fee. The project had raised a staggering fifty thousand dollars in under a month, given her lots of great exposure, and had gone on to gross over two hundred thousand by the end of the year.

Obviously small-town Montana wasn't Chicago. But from the extensive research she'd done in the last twenty minutes on their hotness, Marietta's First Responders were every bit as hot as the firefighters of Local 32. These guys had a secret weapon that they were clearly unaware of, which could raise all the money they needed and then some. And she was just the woman to point it out to them. Surely it was her civic duty. And if it involved getting her nemesis to pose for her... Well, blimey, that was simply a fortuitous fringe benefit she intended to take full advantage of. That she was almost certain the guy would hate the idea—because it would shift the balance of power between them—just made her ingenious solution all the more ingenious.

She detached her gaze from his—time to plan a strategy. She turned to the guy behind the bar who had introduced himself earlier as Reese.

"Hey, English, what can I do you for?" he said, the gruff tone not exactly over-friendly but not snotty either, reminding her that some Montana men could actually find a modicum of charm without bursting a blood vessel.

"Another bottle of this, please, Reese," she said, slapping the empty on the bar. "I'm feeling extra thirsty tonight."

Adrenaline raced through her veins as she scooped the bottle off the bar and took a hefty swig. The cold malty lager soothed her dry throat and went some way to cooling the fireworks display in her panties as she worked out exactly what she was going to say. And how she was going to say it.

She'd pitched for work before, back in the early days of her career when she'd been traipsing round the magazine circuit in London's Soho with her portfolio, desperate for commissions. Now the work came to her. But it was doubt-ful that any of these guys subscribed to *Vanity Fair* or *Vogue*, or kept up on the latest hot photography shows on the New York art scene. She would have to put her best pitch forward to get them onside.

Licking her lips, she locked gazes with Deputy Hard-Ass again. Time to beard the lion in his den of hotties.

She headed toward the group of guys, enjoying the sensa-tion of something rich and fluid as their heads turned and Logan Tate's wide sensual lips flattened into a thin line of displeasure. Her own lips quirked in an I'm-so-about-to-make-your-life-hell smile.

Game on, Deputy Hard-Ass.

★

"HI, GUYS, I'M sorry to interrupt, but I've been shamelessly eavesdropping on your conversation and I think I might have a solution to your fundraising issue."

The smoky, slightly snooty British voice and the spark of mischief in mossy green eyes sent Logan's here-comes-trouble radar right through the roof. He hadn't expected to lay eyes on Charlotte Foster again. Had only just worked off all the sexual frustration caused by their first meeting on Highway 89 by shucking and splitting bales for the pregnant cows on the ranch for three solid hours.

And now the sweaty backbreaking work had been for

nothing, because the sexual tension snapping in the air had put him right back where he had left off the last time he'd laid eyes on her, and her tight little butt, swinging out of view past Our Lady of the Angels on 4th Street.

"Sugar, you can interrupt me anytime," his brother Lyle announced, rolling out the easygoing grin he always had ready to charm any woman old enough to wear a bra and young enough to have a pulse. "Lyle Tate, at your service."

"Pleased to meet you, Lyle. Charlotte Foster." The bane of his existence took his brother's hand and gave it a firm shake. "But my *friends* call me Charlie," she said, making it clear she didn't consider Logan to be one of them. "Are you any relation to Deputy Tate here?"

"So you've met my brother, huh?" Lyle sent a mocking look Logan's way. And the muscle in Logan's jaw tightened. When was his brother going to let go of her hand?

"I sure hope you won't hold it against me, Charlie," his brother said, clearly picking up on the tension and deciding to increase it.

Charlotte laughed, a throaty, husky laugh that sent every last one of Logan's pulse points into overdrive. "Well, that all depends," she said, the naughty smile a dare aimed exclusively at him. "On whether you plan to arrest me or not."

"Logan arrested you? What for?" Lyle did his appalled look and staggered back clutching his chest—which was obviously supposed to be hilarious.

Logan was not amused. He still hadn't forgiven his kid

brother for failing to pick up a damn phone in the last four days.

"Was it for being gorgeous without a license?" his brother said, answering his own question, and Logan's temper kicked up to critical.

He opened his mouth, ready to tell Lyle to back the hell off, when Kyle Cavasos beat him to it.

"Lyle, quit flirting for two seconds so we can hear what Miss Foster has to say." He reached out a hand to Charlotte, too. "Hey there, I'm Kyle Cavasos, one of the local firemen."

"Hi, nice to meet you." Charlotte shook his hand. "Kyle and Lyle, that could get confusing," she said, checking out his brother and the local firefighter who spent way too much time in the local gym. Not something Logan had noticed until right this second as Charlotte's gaze lingered on the overdeveloped pecs stretching the guy's Marietta Fire Department T-shirt.

"Not really, sugar," Lyle jumped right back in. "I'm way younger and much better looking."

"Quit it, Lyle," Jonah Clark got straight to the point in his usual way. The search-and-rescue pilot was not a big talker, but it seemed he'd finally managed to shut his brother up, when he said to Charlotte as they all looked on, "What's your plan, Miss Foster?"

"Before I get to that," she said. "Can I ask you a bit more about the project? And how much you need to raise and in what time frame?"

"So your shameless eavesdropping didn't tell you that?" Logan said, not getting a good feeling about this woman's sudden interest in Harry's House. Or the fact that a part of him had actually been pleased to see her when he'd spotted her across the bar. Hadn't he already decided this woman was bad news?

"Not precisely, unless I'm right in thinking you have to raise upward of fifty grand in less than ninety days," Charlotte replied, not sounding remotely ashamed that she had obviously listened in to a lot of their conversation.

"That's about the size of it, all right," Todd Harris remarked. The local Forest Ranger had moved to Marietta a couple of years ago from Chicago but was as invested in the community now as any of them. "The whole town's been working toward getting Harry's House up and running by the end of this year—it's an after-school program for kids who want enrichment classes or tutoring, or who just need a safe space."

The quietly spoken words had Logan sobering. He rubbed his thumb over the spot on his chest instinctively. However much trouble Charlotte Foster might be, he needed to listen to her suggestion with an open mind. This project was important, maybe more important to him than to most of the other guys in this bar, because he knew exactly how bad things could get, if a kid didn't have that safe space when they needed it.

"We just had a Bake-Off that raised over thirty grand,"

Todd continued, and Logan shoved his hand into his pocket, determined to push the dark memories back where they belonged. That was all ancient history. He'd survived. Harry's House wasn't about him and what had happened to him as a kid—because no one knew about that, thank Christ.

Lyle caught his eye and then looked away, unsettling Logan. For a moment there, his kid brother had actually looked serious. Then again, why wouldn't he? Harry had been a friend of Lyle's in high school and they'd worked together at the Fire Station when Lyle wasn't on Smoke Jumper duty. And for all his horsing around, Lyle understood how important it was to honor Harry's memory just like the rest of them.

"The site engineer hit us with some bad news after his first inspection yesterday," Todd continued. "The structure has drainage problems, which is going to mean some major investment up front, which we weren't expecting and which the money raised so far isn't going to cover."

"So where does the ninety days come in?" Charlie asked.

"The house was gifted to the community on the understanding we'd have it up to code by a certain date. They gave us ninety days to get the work done. We don't meet that target and we're screwed. We figured…" Todd indicated the group with his thumb "…all of us. That as Marietta's First Responders it was way past time we stepped up to the plate and did something. We all knew Harry. He was an amazing guy. Always willing to lend a hand. Nothing was ever too much trouble for him. He was the first guy who I spoke to when I arrived here in town."

"How did he die?" she said.

"He got taken out by a hit-and-run on Highway 89 just after the canyon bend while changing a tire for an elderly couple. And he died in the ER at Marietta Regional Hospital later that night."

Logan felt the guilt engulf him, the silence in the bar heavy with their combined grief.

"He sounds like a very special young man," Charlotte said, sounding genuinely moved. But then she looked directly at him—and the familiar jolt of arousal was joined by a powerful sense of connection. Had she guessed, that the spot where Harry had died was the same stretch of road where he had insisted on picking her up? "A special young man who deserves to have his legacy honored," she added. And the weird moment of connection was gone. "I have an answer, which I think could get you the money you need in the time you need it," she continued. "But you have to keep an open mind. Because what I'm going to suggest may be a bit outside your comfort zones." Her gaze drifted over all of them, but when it stopped on him, he could see the challenge in her eyes, and he did not like it one bit.

"Don't keep us in suspense any longer," Lyle said, his flirtatious grin breaking the moment of melancholy. "What have you got in mind? Because whatever it is, it has to be better than Kurt Mayall's lame suggestion of a sponsored three-legged race down the middle of Main Street."

The other guys laughed, even Kurt, who had made the suggestion out of pure desperation. Everyone except Logan, who had the distinct impression that whatever Charlotte Foster was about to suggest, he was not going to like it.

"Okay, to lay the groundwork: I'm a photographer. A professional photographer. I did a charity commission last year in Chicago that earned over fifty grand in less than a month and eventually a great deal more than that. And you guys ..." She stared at them all in turn, the appreciation in her eyes surprisingly dispassionate—until her gaze landed on him, and he felt it burn. "You guys would definitely qualify for a similar project."

"Hell, you're not *the* Charlotte Foster. The one who did that photo-essay on the final shift at the Penn Ridge Steelworks for *National Geographic*?" Todd asked.

"That's right, that's me," she said, a pleased smile bursting over her face and making him wonder for the first time exactly how old she was, because she suddenly looked very young—a lot younger and less smart-assed than her smoky voice and provocative behavior had suggested up to this point.

"You really captured the essence of what it meant to those guys having to give up a job that defined who they were," Todd added, sounding more lyrical than Logan had ever heard him. He might have guessed the guy would be a

National Geographic nut. The man was a Forest Ranger, so being interested in nature probably went with the job description. But who knew he had an opinion on photographic art?

"Thank you," she said, clearly pleased and even a little embarrassed with the praise, the light flush on her cheeks making her seem oddly vulnerable for a moment. Logan would have been charmed except that her not being just another tourist snapping off shots for her Instagram account, the way he'd assumed, only made her more dangerous.

"Get to the point, Charlotte. What project do we qualify for?" he said, ignoring the sharp looks from some of the other guys as they took exception to his pissed-off tone. If they'd been on a knife-edge of sexual tension for four solid hours—and this woman was the cause—they could tell him to lighten up. Until then, they could get lost.

"How would you feel…" she hesitated, the sparkle of humor in those emerald eyes making her heart-shaped face look even more arresting "…about all posing for a nude calendar shoot for me?"

What the ever-loving fuck?

Logan was so shocked he was struck dumb.

From the coughing sounds, as a couple of the other guys choked on their brews, and still more hissed cusswords under their breath, he knew he wasn't the only one.

From his earlier run-in with her, he'd expected something wild. If nothing else Charlotte Foster had balls. He could almost admire that about her.

But this went way past wild to totally fricking nuts.

"Damn it, Charlie, that's genius. I love it." Lyle was the first one to manage a response. And being Lyle, it was totally the wrong one. "Count me in," he added, the wicked glint of mischief in his eyes matching Charlotte's.

"Hang on just a minute, little bro, you are not serious?" Logan managed, finally downgrading his shock enough to speak.

"Why not?" Lyle said, all nonchalant like, as if he had just agreed to play checkers for an afternoon with the ladies at Nell's Cut and Curl, not strip jaybird naked for ten bucks a pop.

"Why *not*?" Logan's blood pressure climbed into the red zone. Damn it all to hell and back—so now his troublesome kid brother was joining forces with the crazy lady. Could this actually get any worse? "You really want to take your clothes off so everyone in the whole wide world can check out your junk?"

Why should this even surprise him? From the way Lyle charmed every woman he met, there probably weren't that many who weren't already on a first-name basis with his brother's dick.

"Hey, there's nothing wrong with my junk, bro," Lyle said, actually sounding offended.

Charlotte raised her hands as the two of them squared off. "Chill out, lads. No junk viewing will be required. What we're talking about here is *discreet* nudity."

"How discreet?" Jonah asked, looking as uncomfortable about the prospect as every other guy in the room, bar Lyle. Who—on top of all his other sins against seriousness—was clearly a goddamn exhibitionist.

"Here, I can show you." She whipped her cell phone out of her back pocket, scrolled through a few things, and then held it out. "These are some of the shots from the Local 32 Hot Stuff Calendar I did."

She swiped through a bunch of shots of guys, all shirtless, some with their butts hanging out, stripping out of their fatigues to reveal pumped-up pecs that glistened as if someone had dipped them in a vat of baby oil.

Hot Stuff Calendar! Holy crap, just shoot me now.

"They look real tasteful. I'm still in, even if you don't need to see my junk," Lyle teased, still batting for the dark side.

Kyle Cavasos took the phone as the others gathered round to look over his shoulder. "How much did you say this earned?" he said, still sounding reluctant, but not nearly reluctant enough for Logan's liking.

Kyle wasn't seriously considering going to the dark side too was he? He would have said the guy was the least likely of all of them to go for a dumb idea like this. He'd kept a real low profile ever since moving to town after a stint in the Marines, to the point that he'd turned down an award for bravery a few months back, just to avoid getting his picture in the local paper. The guy had put in a lot of hours at Harry's House already fixing stuff up, which was how Logan and the others had gotten to know him, because he hardly ever hung out in town. Surely a guy who had virtually no social life wasn't going to want to strip off for strangers?

"It made fifty grand. Your target. In less than a month," Charlotte announced, proudly. "And that's fifty grand in profit after the print and marketing fees are taken off. Obviously I'd be happy to waive my fee."

"You'd do that? Why?" Todd sounded suspicious.

Even if he was a fan of Charlotte's work, the guy was no fool. Logan didn't know much about Todd's time on the force in Chicago—it wasn't something the guy ever talked about—but when he'd arrived in Marietta, he'd been pretty burnt out. Even now he was a fairly jaded guy. Logan wanted to applaud him.

"Apart from the fact that it's a worthy cause." Charlotte met Todd's gaze head on and without flinching. "I'm not going to lie, I'd love to use some of the shots on my website and blog, with your permission of course," she said, her no-nonsense tone one hundred percent sincere. "And if the calendar's a success...and I know it will be with me behind the camera and you guys in front of it...then the added exposure won't do my career or the prospects for a book I'm currently working on any harm at all," she continued, with total honesty. "But I can guarantee you that every shot I take will be the very best shot it can be. And one hundred percent tasteful while also being fun. I don't compromise on my work. Ever. I may not have known Harry and I may have only arrived in your town four hours ago, but if you guys decide to go with this idea, I will be fully invested in delivering something incredible—that each and every one of us here can be proud of."

Her skin had flushed as she spoke, and even Logan was convinced by the impassioned speech. Whatever reasons she may have had for suggesting this dumb idea in the first place, she would be committed to making it work.

He still wasn't on board, though.

"How are we going to sell a calendar in spring?" he said, prepared to nip this thing in the bud with cold hard logic. "Which is what we'd need to be doing to meet our ninety-day target."

"We can make it a term-time calendar, running August to July for a first print run," she said without even missing a beat. "Given your ages and your fabulously macho professions, believe me, this is going to sell very well with the college demographic. If we get a designer on board, they can reconfigure it for next year and we can do a new print run in January. Plus I'd suggest doing a stud-of-the-week shot in the lead-up to the launch. We can promo it on social media and put him on posters, cards, mouse mats, mugs, et cetera, which could drive pre-sales figures for the calendar itself, but also supply an early revenue stream, so you can add it to your Bake-Off total and get any structural work on the House underway."

"Charlie, you are a genius. Can I be Mr. Fourth-of-July? With the Stars and Stripes shielding my junk?" Lyle said, still joking around, while everyone else fell silent, no doubt mulling over the horrifying prospect of being stud-of-the-week.

"I'm not getting butt naked outdoors for anyone, especially in March. But shirtless I could do," Todd said, breaking the silence first, once again using more words than Logan was used to hearing him string together in one go. "For Harry."

"Way to go, Todd." Lyle high-fived the Forest Ranger. "Anyone else willing to freeze their nipples off for charity? And for Harry?" Lyle added. A couple of the other guys followed Todd's lead and agreed to the project, his kid brother's humor and enthusiasm proving infectious.

As infectious as a damn wiener rash, Logan thought bitterly.

It was all downhill from there. With Lyle and Charlotte pimping the project for all they were worth—they took a vote. Nine in favor, with him, Jonah Clark, and Kyle abstaining. Logan figured Kyle's abstention had something to do with the prospect of having his naked pecs pasted all over social media from the way the guy had stiffened right up when Charlotte had mentioned it.

The motion was passed.

Logan was just getting to grips with the prospect of having to do this thing, when Charlotte dropped her second bombshell.

"This is fantastic, guys," she said, positively beaming with excitement. "If I could take all your contact details now—" she whipped her cell out again "—I'll be in touch in the next couple of days to arrange your shoot dates. Once we've nailed down a schedule, I'll talk with the beauty salon I passed on Main Street to see if they'll donate free treatments to get you prepped for your shots."

"Free treatments for what?" Logan said, the urge to give Little Miss Troublemaker a damn good spanking starting to get the better of him again. He hadn't failed to see the smug half-smile aimed at him when the vote had gone her way.

She might be dedicated to this project, but this whole campaign had payback written all over it. Payback for their earlier altercation. Payback that he was increasingly determined to make her suffer for. Somehow.

"Because I draw the line at getting my hair and makeup done," he said, satisfied when he heard a chorus of agreement from the other guys.

All except Lyle, of course, who couldn't resist another dumb joke at his expense. "Stop being such an old man. Everyone knows real men use guyliner these days."

Logan ignored him, well used to his brother trying to get a rise out of him. The fact that Lyle never took a damn thing seriously could be annoying as hell at times, but his kid brother's optimism and enthusiasm, which was the flip side of his dumb sense of humor, was also one of the things that had seen Logan through some of the darkest days of his childhood—so he never got too worked up about it. Charlotte though, and the way she seemed to be able to challenge his cast-iron control without even trying, was not nearly as easy to dismiss.

She lowered her phone. If she sensed there might be a mutiny afoot, she didn't look concerned, just confused. "It's okay, no need for hair and makeup or guyliner, the rugged natural look totally works for you guys. The free treatments are just to get your chests waxed."

"What the…" And there he went sputtering again. "We're not allowed to have hair on our chests?"

"I'm afraid not," she said. "The buyers will want to see every slope of muscle and sinew. Get the full Marietta Men for all Seasons effect. And a hairless chest works much better with the oil. You're not scared of a little hot wax are you?" she teased.

Logan's thumb strayed to his chest, as his mind yanked him back to a dark time in his life. And an old panic kicked him square in the chest with the force and fury of a bucking rodeo bull.

"No," he said, but the trickle of flop sweat working its way down his spine called him a big fat liar.

Chapter Three

CHARLIE FIRED OFF a couple of shots of the quaint western storefront on Main Street that housed Main Street Style, the beauty parlor-cum-hair salon where the first of her First Responder dudes were scheduled to start operation bare chest.

She grinned as she lowered her camera and spotted Clara Marbles inside, who she'd spoken to yesterday. The feisty older lady, and part-time receptionist, had been more than happy to offer the guys free waxing appointments once she'd got the go-ahead from Main Street Style's owner Amanda Wright.

Charlie fixed the lens cap on her camera, slung it over her shoulder, and headed into the parlor. Only three days after the guys had agreed to do the calendar in Grey's Saloon and already she'd arranged the first waxing appointments and begun to nail down shoot dates. She'd started a blog, set up an Instagram account, had a great chat with McKenna Sheenan—the smart and feisty proprietor of Big Sky Photography—about using her state-of-the-art iMac equipment to do the proofs.

Not only that, but there was already a great buzz around town about the new fundraising project.

Particularly among the women of Marietta—which might explain why the beauty parlor this evening was a whole lot busier than it had been yesterday. Apparently Clara had gotten news out and chest waxing had now become a spectator sport.

"Hey there, honey, you come to check up on the boys to see if they turned up for their torture…" Clara paused to give a theatrical cough. "I mean waxing appointments?"

"As if, Clara." Charlie grinned, enjoying the woman's mischievous smile—they'd hit it off straight away the day before, when Clara had been positively ecstatic at the prospect of arranging to have twelve strapping First Responders relieved of their chest hair. "It just so happens I'm not a sadomasochist like you. Actually I'm here hoping to waylay Lyle Tate," Charlie added. "Did he turn up for the five o'clock?"

The truth was it wasn't Lyle she needed to see, it was his brother. Logan Tate was now the only one of the twelve who had yet to respond to a single one of her texts or emails to set up a waxing appointment. Even Jonah Clark, who she suspected was an even more reluctant participant, had finally given her an excuse this morning for not fixing a date. But Deputy Hard-Ass was playing even harder to get. And giving her the silent treatment. So she planned to use his much more amenable brother to give him a message that he couldn't ignore.

"Holy Mother of God! Ouch!" The manly shout coming from the back of the shop where Charlie assumed the temporary waxing parlor must have been set up had all the women in the place roaring with laughter.

"That'd be Lyle now, discovering the true meaning of pain from Kelsey who I got to help us out with the waxing," Clara said, far too gleefully. "Poor boy's been shrieking like a stuck pig for twenty minutes."

"Stop enjoying it," Charlie said, feeling momentarily guilty. So far Lyle had been the project's biggest supporter. Introducing her around town over the last couple of days— and talking up the project to such an extent that she had begun to feel like a VIP. In the last few days, she had been offered everything from a free veal parmigiana at Rocco's Italian to complimentary fly-fishing lessons from Oscar Jenkins who had approached her in the Western Wear shop while she was getting fitted out with some decent boots.

Although she'd declined both offers, she had been both humbled and touched, not just by how quickly the town had embraced the project, but also by how keen they seemed to be to embrace her—everyone that was, except the man who had inspired the idea in the first place.

No way was she going to let Logan Tate duck out of getting his picture taken on a technicality.

Clara laughed. "Honey, when you get to my age you gotta take your fun where you can find it."

Charlie's reply was drowned out by the round of applause from the whole shop as Lyle appeared, busy buttoning up his shirt.

He whipped the cowboy hat off his head and gave a theatrical bow—clearly extreme pain was no reason not to milk all this female attention.

"Why thank you kindly, ladies," he said, with a rakish grin as he slapped his hat back onto his head. "I don't know how y'all stand that on a regular basis." He stuffed his shirt tails back into his jeans, playing to the crowd. "It hurts like hell."

"That's nothing. You want to try twenty-two hours of labor, big boy," shouted one heavily pregnant woman seated under a hair dryer.

"Good thing you're way tougher than I am, Mary-Sue, or the human race would stop with me." Lyle shuddered as everyone laughed.

A smile spread across Charlie's face as he approached her. Lyle Tate was hot, handsome, and an accomplished flirt—while also being unfailingly positive and optimistic and more than happy to take the piss out of himself—even when subjected to twenty minutes of death by hot wax. She wondered, not for the first time, how he had ended up being Logan Tate's little brother. Because although the men shared the same stunning bone structure and pure Montana blue eyes, they could not have been more different—temperamentally speaking.

Then she thought of Emily, her twin, and realized, perhaps it wasn't that hard to figure out after all.

"Hey, sugar. You come here to inspect the finished product?" Lyle asked, a teasing twinkle in his bold blue eyes as he opened his shirt to reveal the smooth contours of his chest—now devoid of hair. "Wanna have a stroke to check for quality control?"

Charlie laughed at the cheeky dare as Clara piped up from beside her. "Put it away. You're a menace, Lyle Tate. I swear, any opportunity to show off your assets and you can't resist."

"Why, Miss Clara, no need to get jealous—you can have a stroke of my assets too if you want?" he teased, making the older woman giggle like a girl as she shooed him off.

"Actually, I need to talk to you about Logan?" Charlie said, when they both finally stopped laughing.

"Oh heck," Lyle replied as he opened the shop door for her. "Now you really have ruined my afternoon. Is Logan still being a douche about the calendar?"

They both bade Clara goodbye and stepped out onto the sidewalk. Night had fallen over Main Street, the twinkle of stars giving the western-style buildings added old-world charm.

"You tell me," she said. "He hasn't answered a single one of my attempts to contact him."

"Sounds like he's sulking," Lyle said.

"Do you think you could have a word with him, ask him

to contact me?"

"Sure, but why don't..." Lyle smiled and stopped talking. "Hey, Kyle, you up next?"

"Uh-huh."

Charlie turned to see Kyle Cavasos, aka Fireman Hottie, strolling toward them.

"How's it going?" Lyle nodded at the man.

"How do you think?" Kyle shot back. "I'm just about to get all my chest hair ripped out by a sixty-something sadist and her minions." He sent Charlie a pained nod. "Hey, Charlie."

"Hi, Kyle, thanks for coming. Clara's expecting you," she said.

"I'll bet," he replied.

Despite abstaining during the calendar vote, Kyle Cavasos had surprised her, being one of the first to agree to be waxed, even if he had made her promise that no pictures of him would appear on any of the social media platforms she'd set up to create some pre-sales buzz. He'd also asked her if he could wear his helmet during his shoot—which she suspected might be to hide his face.

For such a good-looking guy, he seemed extremely shy about publicity of any kind. But she'd forced herself not to probe. He was willing to do the calendar with a minimum of fuss—that was more than could be said for certain other participants.

Kyle glanced through the glass storefront, and winced as

Clara beckoned him inside, channeling one of Harry Potter's Death Eaters.

"Don't sweat it," Lyle said, but couldn't hide the smug grin. "It ain't that bad."

Kyle didn't look convinced. "How bad is ain't that bad, on a scale of one to ten?"

"One to ten?" Lyle stroked his chin as if giving it careful thought. "Seven, max."

Kyle's hunched shoulders relaxed a bit. "Thank the Lord. I do not want to break down and start crying like a girl with that audience, or I'll never live it down."

"Don't sweat it, buddy," Lyle said. "A few manly cuss-words is all you'll need."

But as Kyle headed into Clara's lair, Lyle grasped Charlie's arm and tugged her down the wooden sidewalk. "Move it, Charlie. Let's get the hell out of here before he discovers the pain goes all the way to eleven."

Charlie laughed as he dragged her into Java Café.

Even though he didn't have the same incendiary effect on her as his big brother, Lyle Tate was impossible to dislike.

Not only was he extremely easy on the eye, but he could take the piss out of himself as well.

He might just be her perfect guy.

★

"SO HOW'S EVERYTHING going? Apart from my brother

being a dick," Lyle asked as they settled at a corner table in Java Café.

"Good." Charlie took a sip of the latte she'd ordered and hummed her approval. "That's good, too." Who'd have thought you'd get a coffee in a small Montana town that could compete with the best they could offer in St Mark's Square or Paris's Left Bank? "I've scheduled nearly all the shoots over the next couple of weeks. Everyone in town's being super co-operative. I thought I might have trouble with the proprietor of Big Sky Photography, worried I'd be stepping on her toes, but McKenna's been terrific. All I need now is for the weather to stay above freezing and for your brother to get in touch."

"Everyone loved Harry," Lyle said simply.

Charlie nodded, toying with the slice of carrot cake Lyle had insisted on buying her—because it was the best in the West, apparently. "I've heard some great stories about him." She'd been waylaid everywhere from The Main Street Diner to the library by people wanting to tell her how excited they were about the calendar, and that had usually led to a reminiscence of Harry Monroe. She now had a picture of the man that had made her even more committed to doing a terrific job.

"Harry was one of a kind," Lyle said, surprisingly somber for once.

"How did you know him?"

Lyle looked up from his slice of cake. "We went to high

school together and we worked together at the Marietta Fire Department," he said, but didn't elaborate, his usually bright eyes shadowed—and it occurred to her that behind the happy-go-lucky charmer was a man who was still grieving, like the rest of the town.

"So apart from giving my brother a kick up the butt," he said, deftly changing the subject, "is there anything else you need help with?"

"No, you've been terrific. Except..." She paused. "I could do with finding a new place to live."

"Bramble House not working out?" he said, clearly surprised.

"Oh no, it's gorgeous and Eliza's been terrific." The Bed and Breakfast that backed onto the Marietta River told a story all its own—of graciousness and romance with a backbone of good ole American hospitality. Charlie had already taken a ton of shots of the redbrick mansion with its wide porch and white trim and its pretty and efficient manager Eliza Bramble. "But I need to find my own space. I'm going to be here for at least a month to get this project done and I'd like to set up my own darkroom for starters."

"I thought photography was all on computers now?" Lyle said.

"A lot of it is, and I always use digital technology for work. That's what I'll be using for the calendar shots. But I like working with thirty-five millimeter in my spare time." Maybe it was quirky and nostalgic, but she loved the honesty and integrity of film, seeing the images come to life in the shadowy light of a darkroom still gave her a thrill. And she'd already decided she would need to take some old-school black-and-white shots of Logan Tate to get over her obsession with that face—and the secrets that lay behind it.

"I don't suppose you know anyone with a couple of spare rooms to rent, short term?" She swallowed a bite of her carrot cake—and had to agree it was luxurious. "I've already checked out the ads in the *Copper Mountain Courier* and there was nothing closer than Bozeman. I don't want to have to get a car if I can avoid it." Because she'd always found that once you got behind the wheel of a vehicle, it stopped you looking at the world around you.

"How about you come stay out at the ranch?" Lyle said with barely a pause.

"What ranch?"

"The Double T. Our ranch. Mine and Logan's. We've got tons of space."

She almost choked on her cream cheese frosting. "You're not serious? Move in with you guys?" That the prospect of sharing a ranch with Logan brought with it a definite hum of excitement did not make the suggestion any less insane.

"Sure."

"But I don't have a car. How would I get into town?"

"Logan works most days at the Sheriff's Office; you could hitch a lift with him. And I spend a lot of time in town too. I do shifts at the Fire Station here when I'm not working as a smoke jumper. And, I'm not gonna lie to you, the social life on the ranch sucks. Plus we've got a couple of hands who live in the bunkhouse—Tad and Ryan. Between the four of us it won't be a problem." He grinned, his trademark come-on-sugar grin.

Four guys? Did she really want to be sharing a ranch with four Montana guys? Especially as one of them gave her goose bumps while also pissing her off.

"And just think," Lyle continued, the challenging grin turning wicked, "no way will Logan be able to duck your calls if he's sharing a bathroom with you."

The mention of Logan Tate and a bathroom had visions of his big body naked and steamy and covered in soapsuds swirling into her head and kicking off a whole new melting sensation.

Whoa, girl. You are not interested in Logan Tate in anything other than a professional capacity.

She needed to control her party-hearty hormones before they partied her into a decision that could cause more problems than it solved. A lot more problems.

She had decided to keep her attraction to Logan on the down-low for one very good reason. The man was a hard-ass. And she didn't do hard-asses.

"Won't Logan be pissed off if you invite someone to stay without his say-so?" she said, struggling for rational, coherent thought, despite her OTT reaction to the thought of Logan Tate naked.

"Probably. But Logan's always pissed about something. I can handle Logan." His eyebrow popped up. "And I've got a feeling you might be pretty good at handling him, too."

"What exactly do you mean by that?" Had she given herself away somehow, to his little brother? The thought might have been mortifying—but it was hard to get embarrassed when there were so many go-for-it-girl vibes pinging off Lyle.

"Sugar, there were enough pheromones coming off the both of you on Monday night to turn Grey's into the Playboy Mansion."

She frowned. *Terrific.* Not only did Lyle know she had a thing for Logan, he seemed to be encouraging it as well.

"That obvious, huh?" she said, because she had never been coy.

"That obvious," he concurred, watching her over the lip of his coffee mug and still grinning.

The fact she and Lyle had no chemistry and he was acknowledging it ought to have simplified things. But it only made her inexplicable urge to jump Logan even weirder.

Because Lyle Tate—reckless, impulsive, way too sexy for his own good and with a streak of bad boy charm that pulled women in like a magnet—was exactly the sort of guy Charlie usually hooked up with. In other words, the polar opposite of his bossy, broody, uptight older brother—at least on the surface. She still wasn't convinced Lyle didn't have a few hidden depths, too.

But she wasn't interested in finding out what Lyle's hidden depths were.

For that reason, hooking up with Lyle would have been so easy. Logan, on the other hand, not so much. Because she did care about his hidden depths. Which was so not like her. Dating had always been a recreational sport for her. Fast, furious, and purely physical. But she was curious about Logan, far too curious for her own good.

"So let me get this straight," Charlie said. "You're offering me a place to stay, precisely because you know it will piss off your brother?"

Lyle's grin became decidedly smug. "Logan's been on my back for as long as I can remember. What he needs is a distraction. And, honey, you distract the hell out of him— which, I'm guessing, is why he hasn't answered any of your texts."

So Logan had been avoiding her for personal as well as professional reasons? The thought left her feeling hot, bothered, and belligerent. Not a safe combination at the best of times.

"You guys have got a powerful chemistry," Lyle continued. "But Logan is above all a gentleman. He won't push, unless you push first. So if you want to hang at the ranch without jumping him, there's no pressure." He laid his right palm on the left pocket of his shirt, raised the other hand. "I swear on my sweet mamma's grave."

He dropped his hands to fork up another generous helping of moist carrot sponge and cream cheese frosting. "And like I say, there's lots of spare rooms, and regular rides into town, so it hits all your happy buttons, accommodation wise." He swallowed down the cake. "Plus the sunset over Copper Ridge from the Ponderosa forest in the foothills on our land is a thing of beauty. I'm thinking you might want to take a picture or two of that for your book."

Her heartbeat slowed then shot into overdrive, because she knew he'd hooked her like a prize trout. She might, just about, have been able to resist the chance to drive Logan Tate wild—and catch him wet and soapy in the shower— but passing up a chance to take some amazing shots? Not gonna happen.

"No wonder Logan's always on your back," she said, not prepared to admit defeat gracefully. "You're a dangerous man, Lyle Tate." Not just smart and sexy, but astute and surprisingly observant too—because he'd just made her an offer she was never going to be able to refuse. Even if she'd wanted to—and she wasn't even sure about that anymore.

He licked the frosting off the corner of his mouth and sent her a grin that said he knew he had her. "And you're a dangerous woman, Charlotte Foster—which is exactly why I like you."

And precisely why his big brother was going to hate having her in his home.

"Have we got a deal?" he said.

"You know we have, you bastard," she said.

He laughed. "I can't wait to see my big brother's face when you turn up."

"Neither can I," Charlie replied—as the melting sensation went molten.

Chapter Four

IT DIDN'T TAKE Charlie long to find out Logan's reaction, because it transpired that when Lyle Tate had a prime opportunity to annoy his brother, he did not mess about.

Less than two hours after their dangerous deal had been struck in Java Café, Charlie was sitting in the passenger seat of Lyle's battered old Chevy pickup truck, with her pack on the seat between them, approaching a beautiful Victorian-era ranch house with white wood siding nestled between a cluster of evergreens on the banks of the Marietta River.

"Welcome to the Double T." Lyle sent her an easy smile as he pulled up next to another dust-covered pickup. "And lookee here," he added as he turned off the ignition, "Logan's home." The grin widened. "You'll be able to get settled in and nail down his waxing schedule at the same time."

Charlie gave a strained laugh as Lyle grabbed her pack. She slung her camera bag over her shoulder and climbed down from the cab.

Something jitterbugged in her stomach. Something that felt a lot like nerves. Except she never got nervous around guys. Not since she was fifteen and had lost her virginity to

Colin Spencer after lights out in one of the many boarding schools she'd breezed through as a teenager.

Get a frigging grip. It's just Deputy Hard-Ass. You don't even like him. And you have a perfectly legitimate reason for intruding on his private space.

She mounted the steps to the porch while ignoring the Mexican Jumping Bean Convention kicking off in her tummy. The peeling paint on the house's siding and the dusty old swing hooked to the porch rafters—which looked as if no one had used it since the turn of the last millennium—gave the lovely house a lived-in but also slightly neglected look.

Lyle gave her a quick tour of the living room—there was no dust here she noted, two comfortable well-worn sofas faced a majestic fireplace with a potbelly stove. A flat-screen TV sat on the shelving next to books on ranching, a few western novels, and an impressive collection of out-of-date hunting magazines. She began to get the feeling that the house might once have been a home, but was now more of a home base for the bachelor ranchers.

Then she spotted a single framed family photo on the mantelpiece. The picture had been taken on the then freshly painted porch, the fall foliage of the trees in the background adding vibrant autumnal color. A tall and skinny young Logan, and baby-faced Lyle barely out of toddlerhood posed on either side of a heavily pregnant woman. She had the same stunning bone structure as both of her sons but Lyle's dancing blue eyes and dark blond hair.

Charlie felt a pang in her chest at the way their mother gripped both boys' shoulders while grinning at the camera. A boyish Logan beamed back at her as if she were the center of the known universe. So Deputy Tate hadn't always been a hard-ass. Where had all that childish joy gone to?

"Is this you with your mother?" she asked.

"Yeah," Lyle said. "Pretty huh?"

"She's absolutely stunning," she said, and not just in looks. The woman's fiercely protective stance and generous smile made her look exactly like the sort of mother Charlie had once dreamed of having. Back when she was a child and she had believed in functional families and other fairy tales.

"She died not long after that photo was taken," Lyle said. "Logan missed her. I don't remember her much," he finished, but his eyes flicked away from the photo when he said it and she had the strangest sensation he was lying.

"What about the baby?" she asked.

"It died with her," Lyle said, the flat tone so unlike him, Charlie frowned. But then his lips tipped up in his trademark grin and it was as if the moment of melancholy had never happened. "Let's check out the kitchen, see if Logan's there, so we can gang up on him."

More questions tormented Charlie as she followed Lyle down the hall toward the back of the house.

Was that where Logan's joy had gone? What about the Tate brothers' father? Had they been orphaned as children?

At least she and Em had had their mother and father around until they were eighteen—paying for the very best boarding schools money could buy while gallivanting round the globe to the crème de la crème of high-society events.

The sting of bitterness dissolved as she walked into the ranch kitchen behind Lyle. Her heartbeat slowed.

Infused with the ruddy glow from the spring sunset, the picture window above the butler sink framed a breathtaking view of the Marietta River winding its way behind the back of the house, the banks peppered by Ponderosa pines. Copper Mountain stood like an elegant leviathan in the distance.

The room itself was big and functional and furnished in a style that wouldn't have looked out of place in a 1950s' movie. A scarred butcher-block table dominated the space while elegant glass-fronted cabinets stood above a worn Formica countertop where a brand-new microwave vied for space with an ancient toaster and yet more hunting magazines. Like the rest of the décor, the cast-iron cooking range and the vintage fridge beside the back door looked old and well used.

"Hey, Logan, where are you?" Lyle shouted. "We've got a guest." He dumped Charlie's pack onto the table next to a half-eaten loaf of white sliced bread and the makings of at least five baloney and Swiss sandwiches.

"Stop yelling." Logan stepped out of what looked like a pantry holding a jar of mayo in one hand and a jar of pickles in the other. Even in his stocking feet, he looked tall, broad, and intimidating. The Jumping Bean Convention went into overdrive as his dark brows shot up his forehead and storm clouds swirled into those broody blue eyes.

"Meet our new roomie," Lyle said.

The jar of mayo crashed onto the polished wooden floor next to Logan's toes with a loud splat.

★

NO FREAKING WAY. Has Lyle completely lost his damn mind?

He'd been busy avoiding Charlotte Foster for the last three days while also ignoring her increasingly persistent attempts to get him into the temporary waxing parlor she'd set up at Main Street Style. He did not appreciate the unpredictable effect she had on his libido—and no way was he letting anyone rip out his chest hair, calendar or no damn calendar.

And now this? Lyle had offered her a place to stay at the ranch? So she could get all up in his face without even trying? What the hell?

But then he took his eyes off the woman in front of him long enough to spot the smile on his brother's face. And knew Lyle siccing Charlotte Foster on him was not an accident. Son of a bitch! His brother had always loved messing with him—but this was too damn much.

"Hi, Deputy Tate, you dropped your mayo," she said, in

her smoky British accent, the bold challenge in her deep green eyes causing a predictable spike in his libido.

Great, so his avoidance tactics hadn't killed that reaction the way he'd hoped.

"I know," he said, but made no move to pick it up. Stepping over the mess, he dumped the jar of pickles on the kitchen table. "How long are you planning to stay?" he asked, keeping a tight rein on the urge to leap across the table and throttle Lyle.

Kicking her out now would just give her the upper hand. And make him look like a turd.

From all the glowing reports he'd heard in the last couple of days from their dispatcher Betty—who couldn't resist giving him hourly updates about the comings and goings of the 'famous photographer' in their midst—Charlotte was fully invested in the calendar and already working overtime to get stuff organized. That meant he owed her, they all owed her, and a place to stay was the least of that—which he already knew was totally how Lyle was going to spin this offer—because as well as being reckless and irresponsible, his brother was also a wily little bastard.

The fact that Logan was still extremely uneasy about the whole idea of dropping his pants so Charlotte could take photos of him naked was equally beside the point. The nudie calendar was going ahead and him and the rest of the guys had accepted they were going to have to suck up any misgivings and get on with it.

If it raised the money she said it would for Harry's House, any embarrassment caused by flashing his butt for the whole of Montana to see would be worth it.

But the fact he was going to have to suck up having Charlotte Foster in his place for the next little while felt above and beyond the call of duty. Maybe he couldn't kick her out—or kick his brother from here to next week for suggesting she hang with them for the duration—but that did not mean he had to pretend to like it.

"As long as it takes," she said. Arousal tightened his skin—and he knew she wasn't just talking about the calendar shoot.

The shot of adrenaline hit ground zero as his gaze roamed over her.

He took in all the things he'd been trying so hard to forget—the petite feet in what looked like brand-new boots, her slim coltish figure in battered boy jeans and a thick cotton shirt, the riot of unruly curls on her head.

His gaze eventually landed on her face, and payback blossomed in his soul at the misty unfocused look in the emerald green. So he wasn't the only one struggling with libido overload. Good to know.

"Pleasure having you with us, Miss Foster," he said, sucking up his displeasure big-time. The muffled choking sound from Lyle at his equanimity was some consolation—obviously his kid brother had expected to get a lot more mileage out of this power play with his new best friend.

Yeah, that's right, baby bro; I'm on to you. And her.

"Why don't you show her to the room next to mine?" he added, rubbing it in.

"Mom and Pop's room?" Lyle said. "You sure?"

"Sure I'm sure. It's the best room in the house." And the best place to keep a close eye on Little Miss Troublemaker.

He shrugged off the shadow of grief and the prickle of unease at Lyle's searching look. He'd gotten over their mom's death a long time ago, and the things it had done to their old man. Of course, Lyle would be more sentimental. Because Logan had always made damn sure to shelter his kid brother from what their father had become.

"Okay, if you say so, Logan," Lyle said, shouldering Charlotte's pack. "Come on, Charlie, let's get you settled in your new home," he added, still needling Logan.

"You're sure this is okay?" she asked, not sounding so sure herself now.

Logan nodded, twisting open the jar of pickles. "I don't suppose you cook, do you? I'm getting sick of baloney sandwiches. And Lyle's meat loaf."

"I can do a mean eggs Benedict and my Irish stew's not half bad either," she said, but then her lips tipped up in a tempting smile that somehow managed to be both cute and sultry. Damn, had he thrown in the towel too soon and made a major mistake with their sleeping arrangements?

"Irish stew? Great, you're cooking tomorrow," he said, struggling to keep his mind on his hunger for a decent meal until Martha returned from her spring vacation to do her weekly housekeeping chores—and off his inexplicable hunger for Charlotte Foster.

British bad girls are not your style. Remember that, buddy.

"Irish stew it is then," she said. "I'll get some supplies in town tomorrow as Lyle refuses to take any rent from me." She slanted his brother an aggravated look. Her obvious irritation with Lyle made Logan a little less inclined to strangle him. So the two of them weren't as tight as they'd appeared when they'd walked in together?

"I told you, sugar, we're not taking your money," Lyle said.

"No rent," Logan confirmed, for once him and his brother were on the same page. "That's non-negotiable."

"Fine, I can't fight the both of you," she said. "And I don't mind cooking occasionally so I don't feel like a freeloader."

How could she come up with the notion she was a freeloader, when she was already giving so much of her time and expertise to the town for free? Not for the first time, he wondered about that prickly independence of hers and where it came from.

"But FYI," she continued, her mouth pursing into a pout that had lots of inappropriate thoughts of biting and sucking that full bottom lip flowing into his head, "I'm not taking over all the kitchen duties just because I have a vagina."

"No sweat. Logan and I know how to do for ourselves,"

Lyle said as he headed toward the door. "When you cook, we'll take KP."

Charlotte sent Logan one final challenging look, daring him to deny it. He raised an eyebrow.

Like I'm going to rise to that bait.

"You have a beautiful home, Deputy," she said, her features softening and her tone surprisingly sincere, especially considering the Double T hadn't been a home since his mom passed. "I think this might actually work out better than expected…" she finished, the wistfulness surprising him even more.

Did The Independent Woman have a soft side?

But then she walked out of the room behind Lyle—and Logan's eyes became surgically attached to her round butt framed in worn denim. Every last molecule of blood in his brain surged southward.

Better than expected? I don't think so.

Adjusting his fly, he set about clearing up the spilled mayo. Not easy while sporting a boner the size of a totem pole.

Chapter Five

"HAVE YOU GOT time tomorrow for your shoot, if the weather holds up?" Charlie said to Lyle as she unpacked the box that had arrived that morning via the local mail truck. "I don't want your chest hair to grow back."

She'd been staying at the Double T for three days now and she had yet to do any shoots. More importantly, she had yet to get Logan to agree to get waxed. In fact she'd barely seen him. Either he was in town doing his shifts as a Sheriff's Deputy or out on the ranch checking the cows that were getting close to calving.

She heard the shower go on before dawn each morning, in the room next to hers, and after visualizing that big body steamed up, it was impossible to go back to sleep. But she'd never been a great morning person, and so far she hadn't managed to drag herself out of the cozy double bed and pad down to the kitchen in time to catch Logan before he headed off to the calving fields to check on the cattle at daybreak.

The evenings had proved equally sparse on Logan sightings. So far she'd spent one evening watching a basketball game with Lyle—while they devoured the Irish stew that

Logan had snuck in later that night and ate—and another soaking in the huge enamel tub in the bathroom after spending an afternoon shooting pictures of Lyle and the two ranch hands, Tad and Ryan, cutting heavily pregnant cows out of the herd to bring to the calving field.

"I'll make time." Lyle looked over his shoulder as he fried some eggs. "No way am I risking having to go through that torture again." The mock shudder made Charlie smile.

"Where and when do you have in mind?" he added slipping the eggs onto a couple of plates and piling on hot buttered toast and the slices of ham he'd had under the grill.

"I wanted to try out back, on the riverbank. It's private and a beautiful setting. And close enough to the house so you can head back indoors between shots to warm up." She did not want Lyle getting frostbite on any important parts of his anatomy; it might scare off the others, especially as he was the only one of the First Responders so far who had agreed to go the full monty and not just shirtless.

"Private's good," he said, placing a plate next to her packing box with enough food on it to feed four of her. "But I won't need any comfort breaks." He sent her an offended look. "The weather's like Hawaii at the moment."

"If you say so." Charlie laughed at the comment. The temperature had been hovering around the forty-degree mark for the last few days, above average for Montana in March, but still chilly enough to have her wrapped up in hat, gloves, and heavy coat. Lyle though wasn't the only guy who seemed to be fine in shirt sleeves. They certainly made men tough in Montana. "Have you got a preferred time?"

"Yeah." Lyle poured them both a cup of the coffee he brewed every morning that was strong enough to tar a road. "Tad and Ryan are repairing the fence on the South Pasture tomorrow afternoon, so let's do it then." He straddled a chair. "If those two catch me with my butt hanging out and nothing but the Stars and Stripes covering my junk, they'll be ragging on me for the rest of my natural life."

"Fair point." Charlie chuckled as she blew on her coffee. Lyle never failed to amuse her. "Are you okay with Amanda Wright coming by beforehand to do your hair?" The owner of Main Street Style had offered her services as a hair stylist for the guys and Charlie planned to take her up on it.

"The pretty little thing who owns the hair salon?" Lyle's eyes lit up. "Hell yeah, she can mess with my hair any damn time."

They ate in silence for a while as Charlie envisioned how she wanted the light to play over Lyle's torso during the shoot. She hoped she could get him out there during magic hour. The light had been glorious over the river in the last three days. What a shame it wasn't high summer; she could have done some amazing shots with Lyle and a flag in the water. Somehow though, she didn't think even Lyle's enthusiasm would stretch to a dip in the Marietta River in March.

The thought of a hot guy in water brought her mind

spinning back to her predawn visualization experiment that morning.

"By the way, do you know if Logan's going to be around this evening?" she asked, casually, as she gave up trying to put a dent into the huge helping of ham and eggs.

Lyle shoveled up the last of his eggs, the knowing glint in his eye telling her she hadn't been nearly casual enough. "My guess is, he's going to be around tonight at some point. He's done four shifts already this week for the Sheriff and he only usually does three… And there's only so much checking he can do on the cattle till the calving actually starts, which isn't for another three weeks by my reckoning. Why? You still trying to schedule his shoot date?"

"That, and his waxing appointment." She stood to open the flaps on the box that had been delivered. "But I've bought a secret weapon for that."

"Oh yeah? What's that?" Lyle asked, while pulling her half-eaten plate of ham and eggs across the table so he could finish off her breakfast like he did every morning. For such a lean, well-muscled guy he could certainly pack away a lot of food.

"I'll show you…" she said, as she unpacked the rest of the bottles of developing fluids for the darkroom she was setting up in the ranch house's downstairs bathroom. Finally she located the other package she'd ordered two days ago, having given up on ever managing to drag the elusive Deputy Tate into Main Street Style.

"If the mountain won't come to the waxing parlor," she said, tugging the heavy tub out of the box with both hands. "The waxing parlor will have to come to the mountain." She dumped the professional waxing kit she'd ordered from Amanda Wright's beauty product supplier onto the table with a resounding thud. "Logan's chest hair is mine, tonight!"

Lyle tipped his chair back and hooted with laughter. "Hot damn. Logan is so screwed."

Charlie bit down on the surge of arousal at Lyle's choice of words.

Nope, not gonna happen.

Time to dial down on her excitement at the prospect of having Logan and his magnificent chest at her mercy this evening. She was only offering him a personal waxing service for the good of the project—and to satisfy her own desire to photograph the man. There would be no screwing going on, of any description. Because she was not about to let their insane chemistry get in the way of either of those objectives.

"Aw hell." The front legs of Lyle's chair thudded back to earth as the chuckling cut off abruptly. "I'm playing at FlintWorks tonight." He actually looked dejected about the regular guitar date she'd heard him practicing for last night while she was lounging in her bath. "Can't believe I'm gonna miss seeing you torture Logan."

"Don't worry." Charlie smiled. "I plan to take photos."

★

CHARLIE WAS FEELING considerably less excited by eight o'clock that evening after spending a whole day at the ranch house, lying in wait for her victim.

At least it had been a productive day. She fitted the infrared bulb in the light fixture on her brand-new darkroom. Dusting off her jeans, she stood back to admire the result of six hours' hard work. With the developing trays and fluids set up on the tabletop Lyle had helped her install over the small tub, alongside the old enlarger she'd borrowed from Big Sky Photography and some plywood boards duct-taped over the bathroom's one window, she was all ready to get started.

The only problem was, the guy she wanted to photograph still hadn't materialized. What were the chances he was going to duck out of appearing today? All day? She headed into the kitchen to put together something for supper. She planned to be ready for him when he finally appeared. Ready with her home-waxing kit and a nutritious and delicious meal to lull him into a false sense of security.

The only problem was, Charlie was the opposite of domestic goddess material.

After growing up in a succession of boarding schools, she'd hit the road with her trusty Leica at eighteen, not long after her parents' funeral—leaving Emily behind to rattle around their parents' six-million pound Georgian town house in West Kensington on her own.

Emily rented the London house out now, and from her share of the proceeds, Charlie had been able to buy a chic little Brownstone apartment in Tribeca when she'd decided to establish a base in New York. But she had stayed there less than a month in total since her career had taken off—after her first major exhibition nabbed her a top-flight agent and a ton of commissions. She was always on the lookout for the next great shot, the next great adventure. Her nomadic lifestyle had not lent itself to learning much about cooking nutritious and delicious meals.

Truth was, she'd already used up her one serviceable supper recipe two nights ago with the Irish stew she'd learnt how to toss together while working in a pub one winter in Connemara.

Luckily, though, she knew how to read a recipe book, and she'd found her second secret weapon for Operation Chest Wax in a box of old books nesting in the bottom of her bedroom wardrobe. She hauled out the vintage cookbook from the drawer she'd stuffed it in that morning and propped it up against the kitchen window. Then leafed to the dog-eared page for Crispy Fried Chicken and Mashed Potatoes with Okra—the oil and flour stains on the yellowing pages marked the recipe out as a one-time family favorite.

She dug out the ingredients she'd bought in town. And read through the simple, straightforward instructions.

Nothing too taxing, even for a novice domestic goddess. By the time Logan finally put in an appearance, she planned to have a plateful of comfort food at the ready to schmooze him into her home-waxing parlor.

As she measured out the flour and seasoning, she stared out of the kitchen window—the back porch light made the night look even darker. Locating a plastic bag to coat the chicken pieces, she switched off all the lights but the one in the pantry. Turning on the digital radio by the stove, Charlie twiddled the dial until Patsy Cline's soulful, seductive voice cried about being Crazy from the speaker.

The stars appeared above the shadowy outline of the pine trees and the rocky edifice of Copper Mountain as her eyes adjusted to the darkness. As she cooked, she couldn't seem to shake the fanciful image of Logan and Lyle's mother standing here once upon a time, making Fried Chicken for her boys, and being as enchanted as Charlie by the Montana night.

★

LOGAN WAS BEAT and hungry enough to eat a whole cow. Dumping his hat and coat on the stand by the front door, he tugged his fingers through his hair.

Even so he'd debated helping out Tad and Ryan with the stock check tonight.

It was only a little after eight. And he'd run into Lyle in

town heading to his guitar spot at FlintWorks. So he and Charlie would be alone here tonight.

He'd made this mess, by agreeing to let her stay here. But waking up before dawn and heading out onto the range without breakfast each morning, then taking every damn shift he could get from the Sheriff's Office so he could stay out late into the evening wasn't working. He still couldn't stop thinking about her every damn minute of every damn day. All it was actually doing was making him tired and cranky and even more horny.

So tonight was the night to face the problem head on and deal with it—or he was going to end up falling off his horse.

But as he headed down the darkened hallway, the sound of Hank Williams crooning about his lonesome heart wrapped around him, accompanied by a scent he hadn't smelled since he was a little kid.

His mom's fried chicken.

He opened the door to the kitchen.

Charlie stood over the stove, the room lit by a couple of storm candles on the windowsill, plucking chicken pieces out of a hot skillet as she sung along with Hank in an off-key voice.

A long-forgotten memory sucker-punched him in the gut. Of his mom standing over the stove singing, her golden hair lit by the sunshine of a summer day, and his father tiptoeing into the room and winking at Logan, before wrapping his arms around his wife's waist from behind and making her squeal.

For goodness' sake, Randall, behave yourself. Go wash up.

The sound of his own childish giggles and Lyle's echoed in his head, making his heart squeeze in his chest.

He reached over and snapped on the light switch.

"Jesus!" Charlie shouted as the tongs flew out of her hand and she spun round.

"Why are you cooking with the light off?" he asked, trying not to get fixated on the smudge of flour on her tank right over her left nipple. "You'll burn yourself."

"Bloody hell." She pressed a palm to her breast as if trying to stop her heart jumping right out of her chest. "Forget burning myself. You nearly gave me a flipping heart attack."

"Sorry." His smile felt rusty but cut through his exhaustion—and the echo of old grief. Why did he get such a kick out of riling her?

Maybe it was the flash of heat it brought into those piercing green eyes. Or the way her staggered breathing molded the soft cotton of her top to her breasts.

Look away from the rack. Right now.

He forced his gaze up, to find her watching him.

"No you're not," she said. "I can see that sadistic smile from here, Deputy Hard-Ass."

The nickname should have annoyed him, but the way she said it, with the lilt of wry amusement, made it seem like she was laughing with him not at him.

He stepped around her to get to the sink.

Act normal.

He blew out her candles as he washed up. And noticed the cookbook perched on the windowsill. "Where did you get that?"

"I found it in a box in my closet." She picked the last of the chicken pieces out of the oil and his stomach rumbled loud enough to be heard over Johnny Cash going down, down, down into a ring of fire. "I decided to vary my repertoire," she added. "There's only so much stew a person can eat."

"Smells good," he said, and meant it. She seemed to have lost that prickly edge tonight. Her short curly hair tied back in a bandana, her eyes eager and excited.

"Wanna try out the result?" The shot of heat was inevitable when she picked up one of the golden crispy drumsticks and wrapped a piece of kitchen paper around the leg.

"Sure," he croaked, the heat swelling uncomfortably in his crotch as she lifted the chicken to his lips. Without second-guessing himself, forgetting all his careful plans not to get too close, he wrapped his hand round her fingers and bit into the drumstick.

Peppery spices burst on his tongue, as he tore off the succulent meat. Her fingers trembled beneath his and she tugged her hand away.

He carried on chewing on the chicken leg as she watched

him, her eyes dark and intense—the lust sparked between them like a living, breathing thing.

He didn't look away, because he couldn't. He wanted her. Had wanted her since the first moment he'd laid eyes on her through the lens of his Government-issued binoculars on I-89 if he were honest. And exhaustion, common sense, even the fact that she annoyed the hell out of him most of the time and confused him the rest of it, didn't seem to matter. They weren't pals, not like she appeared to be with Lyle. But then he didn't want to be pals with her.

"What do you think?" she asked, when he'd finished chewing the last morsel of meat off the bone.

He swallowed, his throat thick with the desire to taste her as well as her fried chicken.

"Delicious," he said, never taking his eyes off her. Letting her know he wasn't just talking about the chicken. And not caring that if she looked down she'd see the totem pole in his pants.

"Good," she said. "Because it's supposed to be a bribe."

"A bribe to do what?" Erotic images of tearing down that tank top and feasting on the nipples now poking against soft cotton made his voice so husky it sounded as if his larynx had been sandpapered.

Her pupils dilated to black, and he knew she wanted him too.

"A bribe to let me wax off your chest hair."

He jolted and jerked back, the sexual spell broken as if

she'd just drop-kicked him into the river flowing past the back porch.

"No way," he said, his voice maybe louder than it needed to be when she blinked. "I agreed to have my picture taken for the calendar. Not to get sheared like a sheep."

★

CHARLIE CONCENTRATED ON switching off the gas under the skillet, and getting her rioting hormones under control.

Well, that hadn't exactly gone according to plan.

Logan Tate looked livid now, as well as turned on—which hadn't been her intention. Exactly.

In some small part of her brain, the part that could still function properly after watching him devour her fried chicken as if he wanted to devour her, she had been sure his objection to the waxing was because he did not want to be seen in a beauty parlor. She'd thought it was dumb, but some guys had hang-ups like that and she'd been willing to accommodate it. But from the way his whole body had stiffened as if she'd struck him, she knew his hostility to the idea went much, much deeper than misplaced machismo.

"Can I ask why it's such a problem for you?" she said.

"Why does it matter if I've got hair on my chest? What the hell is the big deal? Because if this is payback for me picking you up on I-89 and escorting you into town so you didn't freeze to damn death you already got payback for that.

Posing for this calendar is way outside my comfort zone already, in case you hadn't guessed."

She hadn't expected the admission from him. And it gave her pause. Truth was there had been an element of payback when she'd suggested the calendar in Grey's that evening. But since working on it and hearing more about Harry Monroe—and having his mother Jodie stop her in the supermarket two days ago to thank her—she felt a bit ashamed about that. Maybe now would be a good time to tell Logan that. And explain the waxing wasn't just so she could torment him—even if tormenting him had been kind of fun.

"You're right," she admitted. "There was an element of payback in Grey's. I wanted to annoy you, but it's not like that now. I'm not doing this to get your goat. My reasons for suggesting waxing aren't personal."

"You still haven't told me what those reasons are," he said, the edge not having dulled in the least.

She sighed, and tucked her hands into the back pocket of her jeans. She could tease him and flirt with him until the early hours, because sex, the desire for sex, was a basic natural instinct that she had never denied. But talking about her work always made her feel exposed, because it was like talking about an essential part of herself. And she never usually let anyone get close enough to know any part of the real her. But from the scowl on his face, she could see she was going to have to get through her usual discomfort and give him something more.

"Okay, why do I want bare skin? The reasons are two-fold. Firstly, it's a convention—not necessarily one I agree with, because I think chest hair is very hot." She stumbled over the words. "But much more important for me, bare skin feels more intimate. It's more naked, with nothing to hide behind. And without the hair I can control the play of light in the shot better. It gives defined lines and contours in the composition. I sincerely believe that human anatomy is beautiful—however hairy, wrinkled, scarred, or tattooed it is. But for the purposes of this project, I want to show strong healthy men in their prime. I want to show that beauty in its purest, most idealized form. That's the vision I have for these images. I want them to be real but also romantic."

He absorbed what she was saying. She felt a little light-headed at the intense concentration on his face, until she remembered to breathe.

He looked away from her, to stare out of the kitchen window. He lifted a hand to his chest, to rub a knuckle into his pec while he considered his answer. It was an automatic gesture, one she was sure he was unaware of. She'd noticed him do it once before in Grey's.

Eventually he turned back. "I'm still not going to do it."

The rejection felt like a blow, and she wasn't sure why. This wasn't personal after all.

"Why not? Listen if you're worried about me doing it, I got detailed instructions from Kelsey at Main Street Style.

Plus I've read the instructions in the home-waxing kit. And if we do it here, you have the added benefit that no one will hear you scream."

"Except you," he said and she couldn't tell if he was joking.

"I promise not to tell," she said, hoping to lift the mood. Because it suddenly felt way too intense. "Please, Logan, this is important to me... And to the project. I wouldn't ask you otherwise."

"I know, but I can't do it."

"Why not?" she demanded. He still hadn't given her a coherent answer.

"Because no one's going to want to look at my chest without the hair on it."

"Of course they will. Why wouldn't they?" she said, her gaze drifting over the contours of sinew and muscle under his T-shirt. Was he mad? His chest was going to be as gorgeous as the rest of him. Did the guy have body dysmorphia? "All the other guys have agreed to do it. Why won't you?"

"Yeah, well all the other guys don't have a scar on their chest that would scare the damn horses." He spat out the words, then let his hand drop, as if he'd just realized what he was doing.

She stared at him. Seriously, they'd had this whole argument because of his vanity? "That's why you don't want to lose the hair? Because you've got a scar on your chest?" A scar that was probably as insanely hot as the rest of him.

"That's what I said isn't it."

"How big is it? Can I see it?"

DAMN IT, SHE is not going to let this drop.

"To hell with it." Gripping the hem of his T-shirt, Logan ripped it out of his jeans and tugged it up his torso. He stood, waiting for her to recoil.

She drew close—then took forever to inspect the mark.

Humiliation washed through him. Even with the smattering of hair disguising the scar it looked ugly. He knew exactly how ugly, because it greeted him every time he stepped out of the shower in the morning and wiped the steam off the bathroom mirror to shave.

Gentle fingertips touched the burned flesh, smoothing the hair away and his pec jumped. The surge of heat into his crotch at her exploration only made his humiliation increase.

Finally the torture stopped and she withdrew her hand. "How old is it?" she asked.

He dropped his shirt, tucked the tail back beneath his belt so he wouldn't have to meet her gaze. "I've had it a while," he murmured, not about to tell her he'd had the thing since he was ten years old.

"I don't think it's ugly at all," she said.

That got his attention.

He'd always had to wear a T-shirt when he went swimming in the creek as a kid. Had made endless excuses about this mark and others, so no one would ever know about what went on after his mother had died. And now she was telling him it wasn't that bad. Was she blind?

"I know it's gross; you don't have to patronize me."

"I'm not patronizing you, Logan. It's not that big. I think maybe you're oversensitive about it. Believe me, no one is going to be put off by that scar. If anything it makes you even more intriguing."

She thought the scar was intriguing? How intriguing would she find it, if she discovered how he'd gotten it?

"I don't care. I'm still not waxing my chest. I don't want everyone looking at it." Because the scar represented his silent shame.

The silent shame he had kept secret from everyone throughout so much of his childhood and adolescence. Not just his teachers, but also all the folks in Marietta, all his friends in elementary school and middle school and Marietta High. Even his own kid brother.

The secret that his father had become nothing more than a drunk. A mean drunk, who used Logan as his own personal punching bag some nights when he couldn't handle his anger at the world for taking away Logan's mother. A miserable drunk, who would whimper and moan and fall asleep in his clothes and wet his pants on other nights, leaving Logan to clean up the mess and cook mac and cheese for supper again while getting Lyle to help out with the chores by pretending it was a game. A useless drunk who had sold off most of the Double T's prime pasture land before Logan was sixteen because he'd rather get lost in a bottle of Wild Turkey than look after his ranch and his sons.

"I don't want to be intriguing," he said. "I don't want anyone to see it." Maybe it was irrational. But he'd spent so much of his life hiding the truth from everyone—lying and pretending that everything was great when it wasn't. Covering his father's tracks—his moods and his meanness—until the drinking had gotten so bad Logan had spent most nights as a teenager dragging his father out of the Wolf Den and pretending to the other deadbeat clientele there he found his old man's endless tirades and pity parties amusing.

He'd once admired his father so much. He'd hero-worshipped the guy as a young boy. The way he'd adored his mother. But Ellie Tate's sudden death had broken her husband and, at eight years old, Logan had been left to pick up the pieces. To hold things together for his kid brother Lyle, who at four had no idea why his daddy shouted so much, and never smiled anymore.

He didn't want people to see the scar—because it would mean all that work and effort, all those lies and half-truths, all those lonely, terrifying nights when he lay in bed, his body weeping from the latest beating—would have been for nothing. If anyone saw the mark they would know his father had once held him down and branded him like a piece of cattle.

The biggest shame of all was that he'd been glad when his father had finally died. Glad that he could bury Randall Tate in the town cemetery alongside the woman he had loved, and never again have to take another cuff, or slap or kick or cussword from the cruel, heartless, broken man he had become.

"If you don't want anyone to see it, we can always photoshop it." Charlie's soft words interrupted the dark thoughts.

"What?"

"It's not that big. I can easily edit the scar out of the finished picture. If that's what you want."

"Really?"

"Yes, really. But it'll be much easier to do that effectively with bare skin."

"I…" He hesitated; he still wasn't sure about losing the hair. Knowing she'd be able to see the mark a lot more clearly and might figure out what it was, and how he'd got it. But somehow her steady gaze, devoid of judgment, had him nodding. "Okay, I'll do it."

"You'll have your chest waxed? Really?"

"Yes, really." He broke eye contact, her pleasure at the concession somehow meaning more than it should. "But I want some more of your fried chicken first. To get my strength up."

★

STOP HYPERVENTILATING OVER his chest.

Charlie stirred the warm pot of wax, checking the thermometer for the umpteenth time to avoid staring at the man sitting half naked in front of her.

They'd set up their home-waxing parlor in the house's main bathroom, and she'd made Logan as comfortable as she could on the chair he'd carried up from the kitchen. It was a big airy room, with windows looking out into the Montana night. But Logan was a big guy, and somehow he seemed to have sucked the air right out of the room as soon as he'd taken off his T-shirt.

His chest was magnificent. Something she'd noticed as soon as he'd hefted up his T-shirt to show her the scar above his left nipple. She'd found it difficult to disguise her breathing difficulties then; she was finding it even harder now.

More than anything she would have liked to photograph him like this before she waxed him, sitting on the chair, his shoulders back, his expression tense, the contours and slopes of that hard masculine body so perfect she could feel the raw power emanating off him.

Truth be told, the pelt of dark hair, that grew in springy curls over his pectorals then tapered into a thin line down clearly defined abdominal muscles was as spell-bindingly male as the rest of him. And she would be sorry to see it go. The burn on his chest that he was so self-conscious about, though, wasn't the only scar. There were several more nicks and cuts, one nasty one on his shoulder and another on his ribs.

His skin was pale after the winter months, but still held the remnants of a tan. She wondered if the Tates had Mediterranean or Native American ancestry because he had the kind of swarthy complexion that she bet went a deep copper brown as soon as he saw the summer sun. She would add some color to his skin for the calendar shot in Photoshop, lose the slight tan line on his neck. But she wanted to persuade him to let her at least keep the scars, all of them, because it was his very imperfections that made his body so physically compelling.

And frankly a little overwhelming.

It wasn't like her to be overwhelmed. But then she doubted she'd ever seen a more ruggedly male physical specimen in her life. The previous men she'd dated had been arty, big city bad boys, who labored with their minds rather than their bodies. That had to be why this man's body was so breathtaking. It was an instinctive feminine reaction to the alpha male of the species.

An alpha male who was currently scowling at her—as if he was not at all happy about what was going to happen.

Supper had been a mostly silent affair, after he'd agreed to let her wax him. Logan was a man of few words it transpired. And as a result the tension had been building between them ever since. At least it hadn't stopped him devouring two platefuls of her fried chicken and mashed potatoes.

That he'd put his trust in her, despite his misgivings, felt somehow significant. So whatever happened, she did not want to muck this up.

She stirred the wax again and laid out the gauze strips she would be using, trying to still the slight tremor in her fingers. What on earth was she getting nervous about? This was no big deal.

He'd already taken a shower at her instruction, but had put his jeans back on.

"Could you undo the top buttons on your fly?" she said, as nonchalantly as possible.

He grunted an acknowledgement.

She checked the thermometer again at the sound of the buttons sliding out of their holes. Ran through the steps in her head that Kelsey had outlined.

"Right, let's get this over with."

Scooting closer on her stool, she ran her fingers along his V. His stomach muscles trembled as she pushed back the denim, slid her thumbs along the roped sinews and tugged the waistband of his boxer shorts down to rest on his hip bones. His skin felt warm against her fingertip, as she ran it down the happy trail of hair.

Heat surged. She could feel his eyes on her, watching, waiting.

Did he feel the heat, too? Why did the blast of connection, which could only be sexual, feel like more than that?

"Tell me if the wax is too hot," she murmured, her voice a husky whisper.

Taking the wooden spatula, she smoothed the warm brown viscous substance over the strip of hair that led from the top of his pants, to just below his belly button.

His grunt sounded even deeper and huskier than hers. But he said nothing as she smoothed the strip of gauze over the wax, then pressed it down.

"Feel free to yell if you want," she said, and met his gaze. "Your brother certainly did."

The intensity in his blue eyes did nothing to calm the riot of sensations prickling over her skin.

"Just get on with…"

She ripped the strip away.

"Shit!" He hissed, the sound deep and guttural. "That hurt."

"I know. Sorry," she said and actually meant it. Up until an hour ago, she would have gotten a certain amount of sadistic pleasure out of having Logan Tate and his chest hair at her mercy. But not anymore. Because she now knew this was the very least of the pain he had once suffered and endured in his life. The hurt and humiliation that had shadowed his eyes when he had let her examine his scar had touched something inside her that she didn't want touched.

Her empathy.

She shook off the sentimental thought—because it was not helping with her breathlessness. She examined the rest of the job as dispassionately as she could in the face of that phenomenal V.

"Only about…" She did a quick calculation—luckily he didn't have any hair on his ribs or his shoulders. "Five more strips to go. If you think you can stand it?" she said. Not sure why she would want to give him an out.

"I can, if you can," he said and she had the weirdest feeling he knew… That hurting him was hurting her too. Not good.

Something had changed between them tonight, something profound. Her lungs squeezed as she stirred and smoothed the wax for the next strip.

Get on with it, Charlie. Before you stop breathing all together.

⭐

HOLY HELL. HOW the heck did women stand that? And why did they?

Logan examined the stinging skin of his chest and rubbed the ugly mark on his left pec, while his torturer packed away her waxing supplies.

He looked as bare as a baby, a rather red baby, but for the burn mark. The top edge of the Double T logo was clearly visible now—just as he had figured it would be. But she hadn't said anything. And the hair would grow back eventually.

Whether he'd be able to forget the feel of her fingers, gliding over the warm wax before she ripped out each length of hair, was another matter. Because on some totally screwed-up level, there had been something erotic about the whole procedure.

Erotic, except for the damn pain. If he'd wanted any evidence that he wasn't into anything real kinky this was it. At least the pain part of the whole procedure had stopped the erection pounding to life in his pants from getting ahead of itself when she'd slipped her fingers under the waistband of his shorts.

Only problem now was, as he watched her short hair fall over her face, his dick already seemed to have forgotten the pain she'd caused.

"We all finished?" he asked.

She glanced at him. And hesitated. But then she lifted a small tub out of the box. "Would you like me to put some aloe vera on your skin? It should help with the stinging."

"Aloe what?" he asked, stalling for time.

They both knew he could do it himself. But the arousal her suggestion had triggered was impossible to ignore.

"Aloe vera." She read the label on the tub. "It's supposed to soften, hydrate, and nourish your skin and reduce redness, dryness, and scarring."

Did he want to cross this line? Could he stop himself?

"What does it smell like?" he asked. "Because I don't want to smell like a bouquet of roses."

Not true, if her hands were rubbing the lotion in, he didn't care what he smelled like. It would be worth it.

She unscrewed the lid and sniffed, then held out the jar.

He took a deep breath in, and caught nothing but the tantalizing scent of her.

"Okay?" she asked.

He nodded.

Scooping out a handful of the gel, she rubbed it into her palms, then moved closer. Her fingers began at his waistline. Heat pooled in his crotch—warm and fluid and uncontrolled—as she massaged in the gel. He dropped his head back against the chair, stared at the light fixture above his head and concentrated on keeping his mind the hell out of his pants. Not easy when he had just agreed to a much greater torture than getting his chest hair ripped out at the roots.

Her fingers, strong and bold, roamed over his abdomen, trailing up his ribs, and massaging his pecs. He jolted as her thumb stroked over the scar, touching the old burn. No one had ever touched the mark before, not specifically. He opened his eyes, forced himself to watch her reaction.

Her gaze met his, almost as if she'd sensed him watching her. Shock reverberated through him first. That wasn't disgust or pity he could see in her face. She was turned on. As turned on as he was. Her arousal reflected in the dark dilated pupils, the flush of awareness on her skin.

Shifting forward, he cradled her cheeks in his hands.

To hell with it, he wanted to taste her, just once.

Her hands rested on his waist, but she didn't object, didn't push him away as he brought her mouth to his, and whispered over her lips.

"What's going on between you and my brother?" He needed to know, to be sure, the spike of jealousy torturing him.

Her gaze became heavy-lidded, the provocative smile spurring him on. "Nothing. We're pals. That's all."

"Good." The final thread on his control snapped like a high-tension cable.

She opened for him, letting him plunder, letting him explore the sultry taste of her. The pounding in his crotch became unbearable. The sting from the waxing making his skin all the more sensitive. He tilted her face, angling her mouth to take the kiss deeper, to possess more. To possess all of her.

She delved back, her hunger as wild and unapologetic as his own. Her fingers plunged into his hair and massaged his scalp.

Sensation rippled over his skin, the liquid weight in his groin deepening. The pounding heat becoming a throbbing wound.

Her taste was sultry and spicy and yet so subtle. He drew back first, rested his forehead on hers. He listened to her staggered breathing, absorbed the light brush of her breath on his jaw.

"Not a good idea," he managed, round the ball of lust blocking off his air supply. Although for the life of him, he couldn't figure out why.

She pulled back abruptly, forcing him to let her go.

"Shame," she said, not disputing his assertion. "Your lip action is impressive."

He chuckled, the bark of amusement a relief.

Jesus, she was a piece of work.

But as she finished packing up the supplies, his amusement died.

She handed him the tub of gel. "Put that on, if you need it. And let me know when you can do your shoot? Next week would be good, before the hair grows back."

He grasped her wrist as she turned to go, feeling irrationally annoyed by the clinical shift from siren to businesswoman.

"You're going to pretend that didn't happen? What's the deal?"

She tugged her wrist out of his. "You tell me?" she said. Then turned and walked out of the room.

He sat in the bathroom, frustrated and annoyed and feeling like the biggest dumbass on the planet. And he wasn't sure why.

Was it for starting something he knew he shouldn't finish?

Or not finishing something he should never have started?

Because his dick was telling him one thing, and his head was telling him something else. And neither one of them was making any sense at all.

And he had a bad feeling that staying the heck out of

Charlotte Foster's orbit for the next month was not going to be enough to cure the hunger powering through his body now he'd tasted exactly what he was missing.

Chapter Six

"EXCELLENT, NOW TURN into the light." Charlie lifted the camera and fired off another barrage of shots. "Wonderful, you look super hot."

"Uh-huh. Well, the camera lies." Lyle sent her a rigid grin, the smooth line of his buttocks peeking out from the fringe of the flag, which draped over his torso to cover his crotch. "I think my nuts have shrunk to the size of frozen cranberries."

Charlie laughed, as she carried on clicking the shutter. If the rest of the guys were as good-humored as Lyle in the face of extreme discomfort she was going to be very lucky. They'd been out in the chilly spring weather for over a half an hour and this was his first complaint. She needed to wrap it up soon though—even if he was more immune to the cold than she was, he was starting to shiver, and that would blur the shots.

"Only a few more poses now; you've been terrific," she said as she circled him one last time, pleased with the play of light over the tight muscles of his backside. With his chest bare, his head up, and his shoulders back, the lean lines of his body spotlighted by the glow of twilight filtering through the trees on the riverbank, Lyle Tate looked magnificent. He reminded her of the young buck she'd spotted on the drive into town that morning, his stance reflecting the strength and majesty of a creature in its natural habitat.

She smiled at the lyrical direction of her thoughts. Somehow she didn't think Lyle would be impressed with being compared to an elk. However majestic.

"Wait a minute. Can I just…" Approaching him from behind, she yanked off a glove with her teeth and touched his shoulder blade to tilt it down. The slick oil they'd covered him with earlier coated her fingertips as her hand glided over his back to adjust his position. He allowed himself to be moved, relaxed and uninhibited by his nakedness.

She checked her viewfinder again, and her breath caught.

This was it, the shot she would use. The bulge and slope of muscle and sinew beautifully delineated as the golden dusk shone off the oiled surface of his skin—the red, white, and blue of the Stars and Stripes perfectly juxtaposed against the vivid blue of his eyes. Excitement hummed through her at the prospect of playing with the colors in Photoshop—making that vivid blue really pop.

"Perfect," she murmured.

He chuckled. "Awesome, but can you get on with it? I need to get my pants on before I lose the ability to have little Lyles."

She couldn't hide her smile as she took the shots.

She saw a shiver wrack his body, and forced herself to lower the camera. She would happily stay out here another hour, but she had what she needed.

"Thanks, Lyle, I'm done," she said, as she screwed on the lens cap.

"Hallelujah," he muttered, wrapping the flag around his waist and dancing across the back lawn toward the house.

She laughed as she looped the camera strap over her shoulder. But as her head came up to follow Lyle's mad dash to save all the little Lyles currently freezing in his nuts, she caught sight of Logan standing on the back porch.

"Get out of my way, bro, popsicle coming through," Lyle shouted as he shot past his brother and dived into the house to head for a long hot shower.

The screen door slammed.

Charlie's smile died as she packed the camera into its case, and collapsed the tripod she'd used at the start of the shoot.

Where had Logan come from? How long had he been watching the shoot? And why did he look pissed off? She hadn't seen him since the waxing incident yesterday evening. Had assumed he'd be out this evening, like he had been every other evening except yesterday—especially after the disastrous end to their impromptu kiss.

Despite her indignation, she felt self-conscious as she mounted the steps to the back porch, his accusatory stare doing nothing to cool the heat spreading up her torso, or the kick of her heart against her rib cage at the memory of that stupid kiss.

She might not know much about love and commitment and long-term relationships, but she knew about sexual chemistry—and the hot glare of it that had flared the moment their lips had touched had been entirely mutual. But while she'd been willing to run with it, to see where it led. He hadn't. He'd slapped her down instead. Made her feel needy and desperate and then left her hanging. And she wasn't about to give him a chance to do it again.

However much she might want to jump him.

Maybe she wasn't the sweet, wholesome, girl-next-door type she suspected he usually dated, but she had her pride. And she'd always been honest about her desires. She did not plan to get mixed up with some uptight, Deputy Do Right who thought he was somehow superior to her.

So she had planned to ignore him, planned to walk right past him and into the house, to check that Lyle hadn't gotten frostbite, when he grasped her arm.

"What was that about?" he said, his face rigid with temper.

She tugged her arm out of his grasp. "What was *what* about?" she spat back, her temper—the temper she'd sworn she wouldn't give him the pleasure of seeing—getting the better of her.

"You and Lyle? You said there was nothing between you

two. That didn't look like nothing to me."

What the…?

She was so shocked by the accusation, her mouth dropped open. "I was taking his picture."

He stepped into her personal space. All six foot three of him. "Since when does taking a guy's picture involve stroking his ass?"

Her temper erupted like the Old Faithful geyser at Yellowstone.

"Back off, you son of a bitch." Planting her hands on his chest she shoved him as hard as she could.

He barely budged.

"*I'm* the son of a bitch? How do you figure that?" he said, his temper exploding with hers. "One day you're kissing me and the next you're making out with my kid brother!"

"Making out with …" she sputtered. She actually sputtered. How did this man have the power to turn her on and make her want to kill him at the same time? "I wasn't making out with him."

"Then why were you touching his ass?"

"I did not touch his ass." Or she was pretty sure she hadn't. "I was getting the pose right. And anyway, you stupid lummox…" She heaved in a ragged breath, and slammed her fists onto her hips, her outrage flaring like a dragon on steroids. "Why would I touch his ass when it's your ass I want?"

"You… What?" He looked momentarily taken aback.

"That's right, Mr. Mixed Messages. I kissed *you* last night. And you kissed me back. Then you freaked out. So you don't get to act all irrationally jealous now about me doing my job, when it was *you* who didn't want me, not the other way around."

"You think I don't want you?" The outrage and indignation were back. "Are you nuts? I've been hard as a rock for days."

"Then why didn't you do something about it yesterday?" she shouted back.

The temper in his eyes turned into something dark and much more potent. "Ah, to hell with it."

Taking her face in large callused palms, he brought his mouth down on hers. The kiss was bruising, punishing in its intensity, with all the heat of yesterday and so much more. His tongue licked across the seam of her mouth, demanding entry.

She pressed her palms against the rigid muscles of his abs, and surrendered to the need flowing through her like hot lava. Her tongue dueled and danced with his, exploring the recesses of his mouth, gathering that delicious taste, her fury with him feeding her hunger.

She shoved her fingers into his hair, gripping the short strands. He boosted her into his arms and she locked her legs around his waist, the heat settling in her sex as she writhed against the thick ridge in his jeans.

He tore his mouth from hers, his blue eyes dark with

torment and croaked, "Bedroom?"

She nodded, then carried on kissing him, her lips roaming over his face, the stubble on his chin, as his wide hands palmed her ass, caressing, kneading. He charged into the house, marched up the stairs then shot down the corridor with her in his arms.

She had a vague thought that Lyle would hear them, but couldn't seem to hold the thought in her brain, because all she could focus on was finally unleashing the firestorm in her blood.

They reached the door at the end of the hall and he crashed into his room, then dumped her on his bed.

"Take your clothes off," he demanded, as he ripped off his shirt. Buttons popped across the floor.

Normally she would have objected to the dictatorial tone, but she was way too far-gone to give him a lecture on feminism and the rights of women.

She tugged her T-shirt over her head, felt the slight chill in the air pinch her already swollen nipples into hard peaks. She kicked off her boots, then lay down to unbutton her jeans and wiggle them down her hips, all the time keeping her gaze locked on him.

He looked magnificent as he wrestled off his boots, bouncing on one foot then the other, then ripped open his fly and pushed down his pants.

The long thick erection bounced up to his belly button—and the firestorm blazed out of control.

She blinked as moisture flooded between her thighs.

Good Lord, the man was seriously hung.

Her breath clogged her lungs. "My my, Deputy Hard-Ass, I'm impressed," she said, the desire to provoke him never far from the surface.

"Good," he muttered, as he kicked off his jeans. He yanked open a drawer on the dresser, rummaged around like a madman, and produced a packet of condoms.

"I've always been a size-doesn't-matter girl," she said, feeling light-headed, the need to gain the upper hand paramount. "But I am currently seriously reconsidering my opinion." Had she ever seen anything more erotic in her entire life, than the sight of that beautiful penis, so gloriously hard just for her?

She reached out and touched her finger to the drop of moisture at the tip, mesmerized when the thick erection jerked in her hand.

"Stop mocking me, you little witch," he said, surprising her with the flash of humor, as he climbed on the bed. "And lose the underwear."

"Then stop ordering me about," she said, but couldn't contain the spike of excitement as she unclipped her bra and flung it away, then shimmied out of her panties. She would have to tease him later, once she wasn't about to be burned alive.

"And stop talking," he said, his voice as raw and needy as the throbbing center of her sex.

She debated arguing, but couldn't speak round the huge ball of lust in her throat as she watched him roll a condom on that magnificent erection.

Big hands grasped her round the waist, then skimmed her body, to cup the heavy weight of her breasts.

"You're so damn beautiful," he said, his voice thick with need, his expression bold and unapologetic.

The approval in his gaze shocked her on some visceral level. Had anyone ever looked at her with such longing before? Such desperation?

Grasping his head, she dragged it up, determined to ignore the melting sensation in her chest. This was just a booty call. A hot, frantic booty call with a man she'd wanted since the moment she'd laid eyes on him. It didn't mean anything.

"Shut up and do me, Deputy Hard-Ass," she whispered against those wide, sensual lips.

"Yes, ma'am," he murmured.

He cupped her yearning sex, and found the swollen nub with his thumb.

She bucked off the bed, sobbed, far too close to the edge already.

"Please…" she begged. "I want you inside me." This was just animal magnetism. The basic elemental desire to find pleasure in raw sweaty sex. It couldn't ever be more than that. She didn't want it to be more.

But instead of doing what she asked, he circled and probed with that devious thumb, then eased one long blunt finger into the slick folds.

"You're so small," he said, the concern in his voice torturing her. "I don't want to hurt you."

"You won't," she said, getting frantic now.

She didn't want him to be gentle, tender. That wasn't what this was about.

She grasped his bottom, angled her hips, sinking into the quilt, drawing her legs up to cradle that glorious erection. "Believe me I do not need any more foreplay," she said.

He lifted his head, and those bold blues eyes focused on her. And for a moment she thought he could see right through the bad girl act, to the fragile child that had once lurked beneath.

But then he notched the head of his penis against her entrance and thrust hard.

She arched, impaled on the massive erection, staggered by the feeling of fullness. Sweat slicked her skin—the exquisite edge of pain overwhelmed by the rolling tide of pleasure.

She grasped his broad, muscular shoulders, egging him on as he began to move, rocking out, thrusting back, massaging her G-spot with the ridged underside of his penis.

Pleasure whipped at her as he established a fast, punishing rhythm. His harsh grunts matched her sobs, as the wave swelled to impossible proportions, driving her upward and onward toward that terrifying edge.

She bowed back, scoring the skin of his back with her

fingernails as she struggled to draw breath, to hold on. But then he bent his head down, and captured one pouting nipple with his teeth. The sharp nip sent heat cascading to her core and the pulsing ache crested at last.

Her cry and his shout cut through the darkness as she crashed over, shattering into a million glittering pieces and falling back to earth.

★

HOLY SHIT.

Logan's arms shook as she milked him through the final throes of his climax.

He'd never come like that before. Never made love like that before. He felt as if he'd been in a war. A war his battered body might never recover from.

He struggled to brace his elbows, so he didn't collapse on top of her.

He felt shell-shocked. The only consolation was she looked shell-shocked too, her hands falling off his shoulders, her breathing ragged and uneven.

Eventually, after what felt like several eternities, he managed to gather enough strength to lift himself off her.

He heard her moan as he eased out of her.

Guilt and shame assaulted him as he flopped onto his back beside her. He stared at the shadows cast on the ceiling by the dying light and waited for his heartbeat to stop kicking his ribs like a wild mustang.

He should say something. Apologize for plowing into her like a Mack Truck. And that was just for starters.

He winced as he recalled what he'd said to her on the back porch.

Yeah, he should apologize for that, too.

What the hell had gotten into him? He'd never ever spoken to a woman like that before in his entire life. And she hadn't deserved it. She'd accused him of being irrationally jealous and she'd been right.

She shifted in the bed beside him and sat up. He stared at her slender back as she bent to pick up her bra. She pulled it on, reached behind her to clip the hook.

"What are you doing?" he managed, even though it was pretty obvious.

She glanced over her shoulder. "Getting dressed. I should probably check on Lyle, make sure I didn't give him frostbite."

He didn't want to think about his kid brother—and he didn't want her thinking about him either.

"Lyle will be fine; he's tougher than he looks," he said, propping himself on an elbow. "And it's not that cold."

The desire to touch her was unstoppable but when he laid a palm on her hip she stood up, to slip on her panties, and his fingers dropped away.

"Do you think he heard us?" she said. She didn't look embarrassed, just curious. He took that as a good sign.

"He's not deaf. And we weren't exactly quiet."

"No, I suppose not." She tugged the T-shirt over her head, wriggled into her jeans.

"Is that a problem?" he asked, trying to quell the renewed spike of jealousy.

He needed to get a grip. Jealousy was a piss-poor emotion. And he wasn't in competition with Lyle—that was all in his head. She'd told him as much and he believed her.

But something about this woman messed with his ability to be rational.

She shrugged. "Not particularly. I just don't want him to feel uncomfortable."

He huffed out a laugh that sounded a little strained. "Are you kidding? Have you met my kid brother? Making Lyle uncomfortable is next to impossible. The guy's so laid-back he's practically horizontal."

The thought made him feel like even more of a dick. Lyle had been as chilled as Charlotte during the photo shoot. There had been nothing between them. The way she'd been touching Lyle had been impersonal, professional. Plus she'd never once looked at Lyle the way she looked at him. With all that heat and hunger in her eyes.

So what the heck had gotten him so worked up?

She sat down to stamp on her boots.

Climbing off the bed, he pulled on his shorts. Ready to step into her path as she headed for the door.

"Wait, Charlotte."

She stepped back and raised a hand. "Don't say it. Lyle and I are friends, and that's not going to change just because you and I got jiggy together." He saw the flash of wariness in her eyes, making him feel like even more of a dick. "So if you're going to go all Othello on me again, I don't want to hear it."

He rested his hands on her shoulders and she stiffened. The shame blossomed like a mushroom cloud.

"That's not it. I behaved like a jerk. I totally over-reacted and I apologize. I could blame it on extreme sexual frustration, but that would just make me even more of a jerk."

Her eyes widened as he spoke—making him wonder if she was used to being accused of stuff she hadn't done.

"Okay, good," she said.

But when she tried to sidestep him, he stepped with her.

"What?" she said.

"Are you okay?" he asked gently.

"Of course." Her chin took on the stubborn slant that had antagonized him up till now, but suddenly seemed impossibly brave and honest. "Why wouldn't I be?"

He cupped her cheek, the delicate skin soft beneath his palm. "I was kind of rough. Are you sure I didn't hurt you?"

She placed her hand over his and pulled his fingers away from her face. The smile was quick and a bit wicked, spiking the familiar pulse of arousal in his crotch. "Apparently, I like rough."

He took her wrist in his. The rapid flutter of her pulse

beneath his thumb contradicted the flirtatious smile and made him wonder why she was so determined not to admit the truth—that she'd been as blindsided by the strength and intensity of their lovemaking as he had.

She glanced down at his hold on her. "I have to go. I have stuff to do."

"Yeah, I know," he said as he tugged her toward him, unable to hide his own smile. Seeing Charlotte Foster flustered was a new experience. And one he kind of liked.

She flattened a palm against his chest, as he sunk his fingers into the silky strands of her hair.

"Important stuff," she said, as he lowered his lips to hers and then nuzzled the pulse point in her neck, where her scent gathered.

Damn, but she smelled delicious.

"I'll bet," he murmured, as he captured her lips.

She sunk into the kiss with him, sucking on his tongue, uninhibited about her desires. How could he have accused her of touching up his brother, when she was so damn honest and open about what she wanted? There was nothing coy about this woman. And that was the biggest turn-on of all.

She tore her mouth away from his, and braced her palms against his chest. "I'm serious, Deputy Tate. I do not have time for another round tonight."

"How about tomorrow night?"

Her lips quirked, the sultry grin making the heat pound

harder in his crotch. "Are you saying you want an encore?"

"Damn straight I do, if you do?" Why not admit it, he was totally captivated by her. The smart mouth and tough-girl exterior, the independent streak she wore like a shield, and her ability to drive him wild without even trying.

That probably wasn't a good thing—if they were talking about a long-term relationship—but they weren't. What they were talking about was the chance to indulge in a few more exceptional booty calls while she was here.

And boy did he need them.

Because she was right, and Lyle was right too, somehow or other in the last couple years, maybe even longer than that, he'd turned into a mean, moody bastard.

Deputy Hard-Ass.

He needed to lighten up, learn to live again. One thing was for sure, his sex life had been stuck in the most enormous rut for as long as he could remember. He was always so cautious with women. Not wanting them to get the wrong idea. And he was always so careful to keep his more basic needs and desires in check. But with Charlotte Foster that wouldn't be necessary because she was as naughty and nasty as he was.

She was going to be here for two or three weeks. A month at the most. Then she would be heading out of town for her next assignment. She wasn't looking for anything serious and neither was he. But she was easily the most exciting, intriguing woman he'd ever met. And she wanted him. And he sure as hell wanted her. If he was looking for a spectacular booty call to blast him the hell out of his rut, he couldn't think of one with more potential.

What could possibly go wrong?

"What d'you say, Charlotte?"

⭐

BUSTED.

Charlie stared at the man in front of her. And realized she had underestimated him. A lot. He wasn't anywhere near as uptight or judgmental as she'd assumed. She'd been keen to get away from him as soon as possible after that mind-blowing sex-athon, because she was sure she knew what was coming.

If you enjoyed sex, if you instigated sex, if you matched men demand for demand and allowed them to use you the way you wanted to use them, it was only a matter of time before they called you out for it.

It was that old sexist double standard. She'd always been unafraid to own her sexual appetites, which had always put her at loggerheads with men like Logan Tate.

Old-fashioned, traditional, domineering, alpha guys with tons of testosterone and not a lot of sensitivity who thought women should be screwed and not heard.

Or at least that's the kind of guy she'd assumed Logan Tate would be.

But the buff body, taciturn personality, and take-charge attitude had fooled her.

Because Logan wasn't that kind of guy.

Instead of judging her, Logan had judged himself. And instead of trying to deny the intensity of what had happened between them, he'd not only owned it, he'd announced he wanted more of the same.

Which would have been great—because so did she—except it left her with another dilemma.

She would happily sleep with Logan again—because frankly what was not to like about having a wild inappropriate fling with a guy who had the kind of moves in bed he did, who had more heft than Superman, who could turn her on simply by leveling that brooding blue stare in her direction and who was amenable to the idea too? But how exactly did she square that with the tender spot in the center of her chest that had opened up and swallowed her stomach whole when he had asked her if she was okay, if he'd hurt her?

She didn't need nurturing or protecting, hadn't needed that since she was a little girl and her parents had shown in deeds as well as words that needing someone, relying on someone, was a fool's game.

She definitely did not want to encourage any intimacy between her and Logan, because she had the feeling under the hot sex god was a man who had made it his life's work to protect anyone and everyone he thought needed protecting.

Unfortunately, that warning voice didn't stop Charlie

wanting to have her cowboy cake and eat him too.

Enlightenment dawned as she took in his intense expression. The only way to ward off any and all unnecessary intimacy was to make it clear to Logan she was one woman who was more than capable of protecting herself.

"So let me get this straight, you're offering your services as my personal stud?" she said, deliberately trying to antagonize him.

But instead of looking annoyed or shocked, Logan Tate surprised her again. He laughed.

"Yes, ma'am." Another rough chuckle worked its way up his chest. "If you think you're woman enough to handle me."

A laugh burst out of her own mouth at the challenging look in those pure blue eyes.

So Deputy Hard-Ass had a sense of humor, too.

Her gaze roamed over his impressive pecs and glided down to the pronounced bulge in his shorts. Before returning to his face.

"Oh, I think I can handle you just fine," she said, the shimmer of excitement obliterating the last of her caution. "In fact it would be my pleasure."

Taking her hand, he lifted it to his lips, and buzzed a kiss across her knuckles.

"Tomorrow night," he said.

The flames in her abdomen flared higher at the possessive look.

"Looking forward to it," she said. Then tugged her hand out of his and walked out of the room—before she gave in to the desire to jump him ahead of schedule.

Playing with Logan Tate was playing with fire. She would have to be cautious, because she did not want to get burned.

Even so, anticipation had the pheromones flooding through her body at the thought of all the fun they could have together between now and when she left.

There was caution and then there was cowardice. When had she ever been able to resist a challenge? Or a dare?

A little danger was welcome if the thrill was worth it. And on current evidence, Logan Tate—all six foot three of honed, flexible, and surprisingly inventive and unpredictable Montana man candy—would be totally worth it.

Chapter Seven

"SO YOU AND Charlie sitting in a tree… K. I. S. S. I. N. G."

Logan glanced over his shoulder at his brother's teasing grin. And groaned. "Get lost, Lyle." He turned back to the French toast he was making for his supper.

He'd expected Lyle to be smug and unsubtle about what had happened between him and Charlotte, but he had hoped to avoid the ambush until tomorrow morning—in the hope that Lyle might have gotten the message after all the noise they'd been making and gone into town.

No such luck.

Lyle patted him on the back. "Stop pretending to be a bear. I can see that secret smile on your face, man. The one that says you just got laid. And even if I couldn't see it, I sure as hell heard how much fun you were having. Admit it, you owe me for suggesting Charlie hang out here. That girl is seriously hot and you just scored."

"Fair warning, bro." Logan glared at him. "You mention her and scoring in the same sentence again and you're going to get your face rearranged." He dumped the toast on his plate. And concentrated on not punching the smug grin off his brother's face.

Maybe he did have a secret smile. The sex had been spectacular and Charlotte had seemed enthusiastic about them having more. Which was all good, because he was already thinking about getting his hands on her again. But he did not like Lyle speaking about her so disrespectfully. She might be refreshingly uninhibited about sex talk—but he wasn't. Especially not where his brother and the woman he was sleeping with were concerned.

Lyle lifted his hands in a defensive gesture, the smug smile getting smugger. "Hey, backing off, big bro. No need to get territorial. Charlie and I are just friends."

"I know that," Logan said, pouring syrup on his toast—while struggling to ignore the renewed prickle of jealousy.

Which was just plain dumb. And not like him. He didn't usually get possessive about women. Both Charlotte and Lyle had made it plain there was nothing between them. And Charlotte had agreed to his suggestion of a mutually satisfying sexual relationship while she was here. And anyway, even if there had been any chemistry between her and Lyle, he knew for all his joking around his brother would never poach. Especially not now Logan had staked a claim.

But the spike of jealousy still stuck in his craw as he swallowed down the bite of toast, recalling the sight of Charlotte's hand skimming down Lyle's spine and getting perilously close to his butt.

Damn, he was going to have to get a grip, because she was due to be taking shots of all the other guys, ten other guys to be exact, in the next couple of weeks.

"Where is she now?" Lyle asked as he reached over to tear off a corner of Logan's toast and pop it in his mouth.

"She's in her darkroom." He'd asked her if she wanted some supper, but she'd told him she'd already eaten. He wished he hadn't agreed to cover an extra shift tonight at the Sheriff's Office. But then again, he didn't want to come on too strong. They had a whole month to make the most of their incredible chemistry.

The thought that she was hard at work developing some of the shots she'd taken of Lyle that afternoon wasn't helping with his back-off plan, though.

Lyle reached for another piece of toast and Logan rapped his fingers with his fork.

"Ouch!" Lyle yelped.

"Go make your own."

"Well, hell, you could have made me some. Seeing as you owe me so big."

Logan glared at him some more. "I'm not kidding around, Lyle. What me and Charlotte have got going on is not your business. And sure as hell not a chance for you to make dumb jokes."

Lyle's expression sobered.

At last, he'd gotten the message.

But then his eyebrow quirked as he studied Logan.

"You do know this isn't serious for her?" he said, sounding concerned all of a sudden. "That she's not going to hang around once the calendar's done?"

Logan frowned. "Of course I do." What did Lyle take him for? A romantic? The idea was so ridiculous it should have made him smile. They'd had one booty call with a view to having more. That was all this was, all it would ever be. He wasn't looking for more. But why did Lyle's searching gaze make him feel so uncomfortable? When exactly had his kid brother started looking out for him instead of the other way around?

"Charlie's a free spirit," Lyle added. "Which makes her great for a short-term hookup. But she is not the kind of girl who's gonna settle down in a place like Marietta."

"Jesus, Lyle, give me a break, okay." Logan put down his fork, his appetite shot. "I'm not stupid. And I'm not looking to settle down. With anyone."

The truth was he had enough commitments in his life without adding any more. However exciting Charlotte Foster was, she could never be more to him than an entertaining distraction from the many responsibilities he already shouldered. To his kid brother. The Double T. His colleagues at the Sheriff's Office. And the whole community of Marietta.

That was more than enough commitments, even for him.

Lyle's face softened and he grinned. "So listen, I'm not going to be around for the next week."

"Oh yeah?" Logan said, trying to sound circumspect but

unable to stifle the quick delighted jump in his pulse, at the thought that he and Charlotte would have the ranch to themselves—and Lyle wouldn't be hanging about flashing that smug grin at him every time he got into Charlotte's pants.

"Don't sound so devastated," Lyle said, his wry smile telling Logan he hadn't managed to stifle his delight as well as he'd hoped.

Logan felt the smile spread across his face. To hell with it. His brother knew he'd gotten into Charlotte's pants and it wasn't as if he had anything to hide.

"Where are you going to be?" he asked, more out of duty than actual interest, for once.

"As if you care." Lyle chuckled.

"Of course I care, little bro; you know how much I love to track your every move." It had been a bone of contention for years between them: that Logan insisted on riding herd on his kid brother.

"Well, just so you won't have to worry like an old woman," Lyle said, "I'm gonna be at the smoke jumper base in Bozeman."

"I thought fire season hadn't started yet?" Logan's heart galloped into his throat. He always hated it when Lyle went off for his shifts during the summer months, risking his life jumping out of planes and into infernos. He'd learned not to let his fears get the better of him—even if his brother was an adrenaline junkie, he was also strong enough and smart enough not to put himself in too much unnecessary danger—but Logan did not want to have an extra week to freak out about Lyle's safety. It would totally take the shine off his planned booty call engagements with Charlotte.

"It hasn't," Lyle said. "But they're running some additional training sessions—I want to get certified as a spotter. We've only got one trained spotter on the squad; it's always good to have more." Lyle dragged Logan's plate across the table and sliced into the untouched toast. "I'll be back a week tomorrow."

Logan nodded. "Okay, stay safe. I'll miss you."

Lyle looked up after shoveling the last of Logan's toast into his mouth. The smug smile was back. "No you won't."

Chapter Eight

*H*ELLO, HONEY, *I'M home.*

Charlie couldn't resist a smile as she stood in the kitchen doorway and watched her hot date for the night slaving over a hot stove. A plaid shirt rolled up at the sleeves stretched over impressive biceps while his tight buns looked glorious in faded denim. The dish towel tucked into his belt and the deep furrows in his hair, as if he'd been raking his fingers through it, completed the picture of a man totally comfortable in his masculinity while rustling up something that smelled delicious.

Was he cooking her supper? She wasn't sure how she felt about that. It kind of made this a date date, instead of just a booty call date.

Awareness surged, lifting the weariness that had been dragging her down when she'd caught a lift to the ranch with Tad after two calendar shoots in town at Marietta Regional Hospital—one with the paramedic Patrick Freeman and the other with ER doctor Gavin Clark, brother of the elusive Jonah.

Whatever. She needed a decent meal. Because she had a

feeling she was going to need to get her strength up for tonight's activities.

She scooped her camera out of the bag and eased off a single shot.

Caption: Masculinity in the kitchen.

The click of the shutter had Logan swinging round, spatula in hand. "Hey, you're back?" he said.

"Hmmm," she said and placed her camera and camera bag on the table. "What are you cooking?"

"Steaks, potatoes, and I thought I'd rustle us up a garden salad." He turned back to the stove and flipped the steaks on the griddle. "Figured you might want something to eat."

He *was* cooking her dinner. She felt the melting sensation in her chest and ignored it. This was not cute. It was just sustenance. And she was ravenous. So all good.

"I'll do the salad," she said, crossing to the fridge. She pulled out a head of lettuce, some tomatoes, and cucumber. Then rinsed and sliced and chopped before tossing together a vinaigrette after deciding the blue cheese dressing on the shelf had about a billion additives.

But as they worked together in silence, the tension mounted. Photographing half-naked hunks all day had put her on edge—until all she'd been able to think about was getting back to the ranch and jumping Logan Tate's bones. Having him cook supper for her was not making her any less edgy.

He sat down, the two plates loaded with freshly grilled

steaks and baked potatoes as big as bowling balls slathered in golden melting butter.

"We're good to go. Why don't you grab the silverware?" he said, pointing her to the drawer beside the stove as he ripped the dish towel out of his belt.

He looked a little tense. Not so good. Unless she made it her mission to relax him.

"Where's Lyle?" she asked as she tucked into the meal—which was simple, satisfying, and almost as delicious as her date.

"He's staying in Bozeman tonight," Logan said, sawing into his steak.

"I see." She savored another succulent bite of steak, the grilled meat so fresh it all but melted on her tongue. A trickle of juice leaked out of her mouth. She lapped it up, aware of Logan's gaze on her lips.

He concentrated on adding some salad to his plate.

"Gonna be there till next week," he said, not looking at her. "Doing a course to earn his spotter stripes."

She put her fork down—now officially full and through eating. However ravenous she had been for food, she was a great deal more ravenous for the man in front of her. Time for affirmative action.

"You had me at 'He's staying in Bozeman, tonight'," she said, unable to hide the flirtatious grin as his gaze met hers.

"Something on your mind, Charlotte?" he said, the lazy smile making her flirt gene go into overdrive.

Who exactly was teasing whom here?

"Something's been on my mind since last night, actually," she said. Getting up from her chair, she stepped toward him, gratified when he lowered his fork. "I'm finished. And that was delicious." She plucked his fork out of his hand and laid it on his plate. "If you haven't finished how would you feel about warming it up later?" She pushed his plate away, loving the way his eyes darkened as she climbed up onto the kitchen table and sat in front of him, her legs perched on either side of his chair. "And eat me instead."

The request was bold and dirty and deliberately provocative.

How would Deputy Hard-Ass react?

Lifting his napkin, he wiped his mouth. "You're a very bad girl, aren't you, Charlotte?"

Endorphins fired through her at the husky tone of voice. And the playful glint in his eyes.

"Take off your pants." He stared at her.

She chuckled. *Oh my God. Did he actually just get even hotter?*

"Now, Charlotte."

She jumped at the curt demand. And immediately unbuttoned her fly. Slipping the jeans off while perched on a table turned out to be not the easiest or most graceful manoeuver, however. Once she'd wriggled the confining denim down her hips, she was stuck fast, her boots halting her progress—with Logan's eyes glittering with amusement at her predicament.

"Bugger!" she said.

"You want some help, Charlotte?" he said in that I'm-the-boss-of-you voice that had once gotten on her nerves, but was now making her nerves vibrate in some very interesting places.

She huffed. "Yes! Could you take my boots off?"

He clasped her hips, then slid his callused palms down to her knees, firing sensation up her naked thighs and into her already yearning sex.

"Sure I can," he said. "But only if you ask me nicely."

"Please, Deputy Hard-Ass." She fluttered her eyelashes outrageously. "Will you take off my boots for me?"

His gaze remained locked on hers, as he tugged off first one boot, then the other. They clattered to the floor. Before he stood up, and dragged her jeans the rest of the way off.

He positioned himself between her open legs. Large hands grabbed her bottom, and jerked her toward him, until the thin swatch of lace covering her sex butted against the thick ridge in his pants.

She stretched back, arching up, to rub the erection. Everything inside her melting with need.

"Take off your shirt," he demanded, the teasing glint gone.

She undid the buttons, taking her time, loving the surge of heat and power as he tracked each new inch of exposed skin.

At last the shirt dropped open to reveal her matching bra.

Blunt fingers slipped under the waistband of her panties to massage her ass.

"All the way off, Charlotte."

She shrugged off the shirt, not easy when he was holding her so tightly.

"Now lose the bra."

Her breath came out in ragged pants as she unclipped the hook. The straps fell off her shoulders and she clasped the lace to her breasts.

Pulling a hand out of her panties, he tugged the thin covering away and flung it over his shoulder.

Suddenly she was naked, or as good as naked. While he was still fully clothed.

"Brace your hands behind you," he said, the deep voice now feral with demand.

She did as she was told, the movement forcing her back to arch, offering her vulnerable breasts to him.

He cupped one heavy mound in a large palm and lifted it to his mouth. Arrows of sensation, hot and furious, darted down as he played with the nipple, teasing and tempting then sucking it to the roof of his mouth.

She couldn't focus, couldn't think, her whole body quivering with need. Then he transferred that cruel relentless mouth to the other breast.

She arched even higher, the torturous play of lips, teeth, tongue, too good to resist.

Just when she thought she couldn't stand any more, he stopped. Straightened. The slow smile that spread across his face one of devastating masculine superiority. She could feel the chill of air on her wet nipples, imagined what a wanton she must look like, sitting there sucking in air with nothing but her soaked panties on.

"Don't stop," she managed to say.

Turning round, he dragged his chair back, and sat down on it. Then clamped his hands on her bottom and drew her right to the table's edge.

He inserted a finger into the gusset of her panties. She bucked as his knuckle brushed against the wet, swollen flesh.

"Easy, Charlotte," he said as if gentling a wild mustang, then—watching her reaction—ripped the delicate lace.

She jolted, shocked at the rush of endorphins turning her knees to jelly.

Who is this guy? And who am I? Because I am so getting off on his caveman act.

This big, bold, brooding man and his pushy, dominant behavior was the opposite of what she should normally find arousing. And yet she had never been more turned on in her entire life.

She didn't have more than a few seconds to contemplate that, before he leant forward and blew across the swollen folds. "Put your legs over my shoulders."

Again she obeyed without question. So not like her. But when he licked the skin of her inner thigh, she could not give a toss.

He nudged her sex with has nose, breathing in her scent, then drew his tongue over her center.

She groaned, her head falling back, her body bracing for the onslaught. He licked with agonizing slowness at first— the long, darting laps, gathering her taste, discovering her weaknesses, and devouring her self-control. Her cries became hoarse, foreign, the spiral of need winding into a tight knot of desperation at her core.

How much of this erotic torture could she stand? The need to hold on, to hold off, became a frantic struggle. Her head thrashed, her thighs trembled, trapped by his hands as he continued to eat her from the inside out. She thrust into his mouth, demanding more, demanding completion, but every time she got close to tipping over that high, wide edge, he would retreat.

"Please just… Oh God!" she cried, her sobs echoing off the kitchen walls as he feasted on the firm nub at last.

She cried out, bowing back as the orgasm slammed into her, robbing her breath, exploding out of her lungs, firing across her skin, and shredding the last of her control.

She came down in slow painful increments as he continued to lick and suck.

Holding her quivering thighs, he drew her legs over his shoulders and then stood. Towering over her, he produced a condom from his back pocket, then ripped open his zipper, and shoved down his pants and shorts.

She watched, dazed, disorientated, stunned by the intensity of her orgasm, and the rapt hunger on his face as the huge erection thrust up toward his belly button.

He tore open the condom packet, flicked the foil away and rolled the rubber on.

Gripping the back of her head, he dragged her mouth to his, the taste of herself on his lips was unbearably erotic before he drew back and then grasped her hips.

She sucked in staggered breaths as he pressed into her, the stretched feeling verging on pain as he sunk in to the hilt. He gave her a moment to adjust to his size, then began to move, thrusting so deep inside her she was no longer sure where he finished and she began. Her muscles gripped, massaging the thick length and driving her back toward another impossible peak. Too fast, too fierce, her breathing clogged in her lungs as she clung to his shoulders, spellbound by the feel of him so deep, so huge.

The crescendo built, higher, hotter, than before. The vise-like grip of the orgasm licking at her spine was stronger if that were possible. Sweat slicked their bodies, the shuddering thumps as the table rocked on its legs matching the thudding beats of her heart as he thrust harder, faster.

She screamed as she crested, all of herself rising up and flying over the edge then dropping down, down, down into the welcome oblivion.

★

WHEN SHE CAME round, it took her a moment to realize the weightless feeling was because he was carrying her.

"You okay?" he asked as she raised her head.

"I think so," she said, disorientated and utterly shattered. "Did you actually just screw me into unconsciousness?"

His deep chuckle reverberated in her chest—the sound as raw and ragged as she felt.

"Apparently."

He mounted the stairs, then headed down the corridor to the bathroom. Depositing her naked body on the stool beside the bath, he stripped out of his own clothing, revealing the magnificent slopes and planes of his body. She noticed he was still semi-erect as he took off the condom and discarded it. The renewed arousal surged through her exhaustion, disturbing her even more.

Seriously? How can I want him again already? If I'm not careful I could end up getting screwed to death here...

He switched on the shower in the enamel tub, flicked across the curtain. Then bent to scoop her into his arms again.

"What are you doing?" she asked, shocked by the care he was taking with her. As if she were fragile, or precious. Hadn't she just proved she was tough—and not the type of woman who needed to be cherished? But she couldn't find the strength to resist as he stepped into the tub with her cradled in his arms.

"We're having a shower." He stood her on her feet, but

held on to her waist until he was sure she wouldn't collapse.

She wanted to object; she didn't need any of this. But she couldn't find the will to stop him as he washed her hair, massaging her scalp with strong fingers. Or soaped the rest of her body, bringing awareness tingling back to life.

"You all right?" he asked. "I should go finish my supper."

"Yes, of course." She nodded, but felt bereft when he stepped out of the shower. She shuddered, reaction pulsing through her veins from the fury of their lovemaking as she rinsed off the last of the soap.

The fury of their sex-capade, she corrected. This wasn't love, just a beyond incredible physical connection. But had it been a bit too incredible tonight?

Turning off the water as it began to cool, she whipped back the curtain, to find him standing with a towel wrapped around his hips. She had assumed he would have left. Had he been waiting for her? Watching over her?

She crossed her arms over her breasts, feeling weirdly exposed—which was absurd, because he'd seen and licked and kissed pretty much every part of her already this evening.

He lifted a towel off the pile in the corner of the room and wrapped the fluffy sheet around her shoulders to cover her nakedness. She shivered as he rubbed her back.

"Thanks," she murmured, stepping out of his arms—freaked out even more by the desire to have him hold her. "I've got this."

"Are you sure you're okay?" he asked again. "You look

kind of washed out." The concern on his face wasn't helping with the deep, heavy thuds of her heartbeat.

"I'm fine. It's just been a tiring day," she said. "I did back-to-back calendar shoots. And then you screwed me to within an inch of my life on the kitchen table," she added, desperate to lighten the mood.

But instead of laughing, he winced. The slash of color hit his cheekbones. Was Deputy Hard-Ass blushing? What was that about? And why should she find it so endearing?

"Yeah, I know," he said. "I'll try and use more finesse next time. I swear to God, I don't usually treat women so roughly."

"Logan, you're not serious?" she said, the urge to sooth and reassure not like her, but somehow unavoidable. "I loved the way you handled me downstairs. It was some of the hottest sex I've ever had in my life." Not some of, *the* hottest sex she'd ever had in her life, but she didn't want to let him know that. Getting screwed into unconsciousness had already put her at way too much of a disadvantage.

He scrubbed his hand over his chin, the rasp of stubble reminding her of the sting of beard burn he'd left on her thighs. Then he stared at her out of those broody blue eyes. "You sure?" he asked.

"Sure, I'm sure," she said. "It's not every day a girl has an orgasm so epic she passes out."

The laugh that left those gorgeous lips was strained, but somehow all the more enchanting for it.

Lyle had been right, despite his dominant, sex-god tendencies—tendencies she suspected were as new to him as they were to her—Logan Tate was a gentleman.

She had a moment to contemplate how much more vulnerable that discovery made her feel when her stomach rumbled loudly enough to be heard in Texas.

He smiled, the slow sexy quirk of his lips making her thumping heartbeat thud right back into her sex.

Oh for... Get a bloody grip, you nymphomaniac.

Thrusting his fingers through his hair, he said, "Why don't you go get dressed? I'll clean up the mess we made in the kitchen and reheat what's left of the food."

"I'm not hungry," she said—because she really wasn't that hungry for food. And she did not want to give in to her hunger for Logan again tonight. "Half a cow was enough for me." She jerked her thumb over her shoulder. "I think I'll just go crash. I'll see you in the morning, Logan."

He dipped his head, in an approximation of a nod, but his gaze roamed over her, as if he were checking for himself that she was really okay.

She could feel the weight of that assessing gaze following her out of the door as she hightailed it out of the bathroom. She felt like a coward as she reached her own bedroom. But as she dumped her towel and slipped under the patchwork quilt, the lingering soreness between her thighs making its presence felt, her heartbeat finally stopped pummeling her chest like a heavyweight champ on speed.

Beating a hasty retreat tonight had been necessary. She needed a chance to regroup and re-establish the emotional distance that was part and parcel of all her sexual relationships. Somehow or other—while he'd been pounding her to orgasm—Logan had shattered her trusty shield, and then delved behind the armor she kept around her heart. If she wanted more spectacular sex without any scary consequences, she needed to rebuild it, which meant getting a good night's sleep.

That weird wobble in the shower had been brought about by fatigue. After all, she'd been running on adrenaline for days now. The work setting up the calendar and the pressure she was putting on herself to do a spectacular job—not to mention all the sex-capades with Logan—had depleted her usually boundless supplies of energy.

Tomorrow she'd be back to her usual self. Tough, smart, and up for sex—without making any unnecessary emotional connections.

Chapter Nine

"EASY, BOY," LOGAN crooned as he rubbed the sweat off Mystic's coat with a handful of straw. He'd ridden the four-year-old Kentucky colt hard that morning, cutting ten more head of cattle nearing their time from the main herd and bringing them down to the calving pens. It would be several more weeks at least before the calving started, but getting the cows all in the right place still provided enough work to keep him and Mystic busy. Which was a good thing, because he'd needed a distraction from his thoughts this morning about last night and Charlotte.

She'd looked so small and fragile after they'd made love. And he'd felt like a jerk. Even more of a jerk than he had the night before.

He still did not know where that pushy streak had come from. Ordering women about was not in his nature. But she'd looked so damn hot draped over his kitchen table, her breasts high and firm and begging for his mouth. Her sobs echoing in his ears as he feasted on her. And seeing that bright reckless light in her face when he'd pushed and provoked her had told him she was getting as hot as he was.

But afterward. Jesus, he'd wanted to hold her, to make sure he hadn't hurt her. The urge to nurture and protect her something entirely new—as new as that pushy streak.

He stroked the horse's flank, then threw down the straw and drew the hoof pick out of his belt.

Luckily, there wasn't anything more distracting—or energizing—than crashing through the heavy brush on a well-trained cow pony while trying to keep ten ornery pregnant ladies moving in the right direction. It had cleared his mind, made him come to some important conclusions.

He'd woken up a couple of times in the night, in his empty bed, and imagined Charlotte in her lonely bed in the room next door. It was probably dumb to want her in his bed—because what were the chances he wouldn't have worn her out even more—but the yearning had been there all the same. If they were going to go on sleeping together—and he figured that was a given, seeing how good it made them both feel—he wanted to actually sleep with her. Because having her in the next room, and not knowing if she was okay, was going to lose him a lot of sleep.

"Good, boy. Let's have a look at those feet."

Mystic lifted his foreleg for him, and he began cleaning out the dirt from their ride. He did each foot in turn, checking the horse's shoes for stones. Mystic stood docilely by. He'd always enjoyed having his hooves cleaned, which was why Logan always made sure to check them after as well as before riding him.

He finished the job, but when he put the last hoof down and straightened, stretching out his back muscles, he spotted Charlotte, standing silently by the stall door with her camera obscuring her face.

The jolt of awareness was kind of surprising, seeing as they'd both worn themselves out the night before. And he'd just spent three hours on a horse exhausting himself even more.

"Hey, there?" he said. "How you doing?"

She lowered her camera. "Good," she said, the slight edge to her voice reminding him of the night before. The wariness in her eyes when she'd caught him making her supper, or later, much later, in the bathroom, when she'd shot off rather than join him downstairs.

She was skittish, prickly, and wary of letting anyone care for her on some fundamental level. And he planned to find out why. Eventually.

He gave Mystic's rump a pat to move him out of the way so he could exit the stall and get a better look at her.

She was wearing her usual outfit of scuffed jeans, a skimpy tank, and a western shirt, her wild hair swept back with a couple of pins. He studied her face, glad to see the shadows under her eyes from last night—which he'd noticed for the first time in the fluorescent light of the bathroom— had gone.

"Logan, I'm good. Stop staring at me like that."

"Like what?"

"Like I'm about to break in two. I had a good time last night. A really good time. But I'm going to have to call a halt to any more good times, if you're going to start acting weird every time we screw each other's brains out."

He tried not to flinch at the deliberate crudity. And tried not to get turned on by it too, even though he already knew that was a losing battle.

"Making sure you're okay is acting weird?" he said, taking off his gloves and whacking them on his chaps to clean off the dust.

"Yes, it is. I'm not your responsibility, just in case you were wondering."

Yeah, she was. But he wasn't going to argue the point with her. He knew a misdirection technique when he saw one; he was a trained officer of the law, after all.

She was going to have to get used to him keeping an eye on her while they were hooking up on a regular basis. Maybe they weren't dating, per se. Maybe this was only a booty call with benefits. And maybe it had a one-month embargo at best. But he took care of the women he slept with. Especially women he'd managed to screw into unconsciousness as she'd put it—and she was a first there.

That was the kind of guy he was. He guessed it was a layover from his childhood—when he'd had to hold everything together while his old man was falling apart—but he couldn't switch off that side of his nature.

And the truth was, he didn't want to. Because there had

been something about the way she'd curled into his arms, the way she'd stood quietly under his ministrations when he'd washed her in the shower that had called to him. And made him realize that even if she wasn't used to having other people do for her, it didn't mean she didn't need it.

From her provocative behavior, and that mile-wide independent streak, he had a feeling Charlotte was a woman who had been on her own for a long time. She was used to doing for herself. But she wasn't all alone on the Double T. He was here too, and he planned to watch over her. But being subtle about it would probably be best until he'd won at least a little of her trust.

Mystic had run wild for four years on a ranch in West Texas before Logan had bought the thoroughbred colt at a knockdown price. It had taken months to get him to even accept a human touch. Obviously Charlotte wasn't a horse, and she'd probably skin him if she knew he was making the comparison in his head, but it didn't alter the fact her skittishness only made her more intriguing for him. And all the more determined to win her trust. And find out what the heck had made her so scared of letting anyone—even a casual booty call—get too close.

"We had great sex. But that's all it was. Okay?" she said, still protesting.

He shrugged. "I don't remember saying any different."

"Great," she said, her relief palpable.

Moving past her, he grabbed some hay from one of the

new bales and stuffed it into the feed bucket roped to Mystic's stall.

The colt stuck its nose into the trough and began to chew.

Logan ran his hand down the soft hair of the horse's snout. He heard the whirring clicks and turned to find Charlotte with her camera to her face again.

Did she know she used the thing like a shield?

"You're taking an awful lot of pictures of nothing," he said. "Can't see how photos of me stroking a horse is gonna be much use for your project."

She lowered the camera, the quick smile devoid of tension, and all the more captivating for it. "You'd be surprised. Hunky guys and horses are some of the top eye candy choices for the discerning woman."

He frowned. "Wait up, you're not gonna put those pictures on the Internet are you?" He'd agreed to take off his shirt for this project, not have his whole life stuck on Instagram.

Her smile widened. "No actually, these are just some black and whites for my own personal enjoyment. Don't worry, if any of them are good enough for my book, I'll check with you first and get you to sign a release form."

He grunted. "Okay, good. Fire away then."

"Thanks." She lifted the camera back to her face and took a load more shots. "Just pretend I'm not even here."

Yeah, right.

He set about filling Mystic's trough and the stalls of the ranch's other cutting horses with fresh river water, and then oiled and hung up the tack. By the time he'd finished putting everything to rights, he'd almost forgotten she was there. Almost. The wisp of her scent curled around him—that sweet sultry combination of orange blossoms and spice mixing with the earthy smell of hay and fresh horse manure. But the clicks of the camera shutter didn't bother him.

She finally lowered the camera, to stuff it in her bag as they headed back to the house across the yard.

"We should work out a time for your shoot," she said. "Before your hair grows back."

"That won't be for a while." He'd checked, on the Internet. It took two to three weeks for waxed hair to grow back. "I'm busy with ranch business. Calving season starts soon." And he wasn't sure he was ready for the humiliation of having Charlotte photograph him. Yet.

He shoved open the door to the ranch house, and held it for her. But she paused on the threshold. "I can fit the shoot round ranch business." Then she blindsided him. "What are you doing now?"

"I've gotta wash up, then I was planning to put some sandwiches together for lunch and..." He hesitated. What the hell else was there to do that would sound convincing? "Then check on the cattle in the calving pens."

"Tad told me you were just in the calving pens when I came looking for you."

Gee, thanks a bunch, Tad, you big blabbermouth.

"They have to be checked on every three hours. Just in case one of the cows goes into her labor early."

Instead of taking his lame excuse at face value, she whipped her cell out of her back pocket. "That gives us two hours."

He was going to kill Tad.

"Yeah but…"

She stepped closer and placed a finger on his lips, halting the stream of excuses he had yet to think up.

"It won't be that bad, Logan. There's nothing to be worried about. It'll just be you and me. You get final say on the shots. I thought we could drive out onto the open range, find a spot away from the ranch, so there's no chance of anyone eavesdropping." Her lips quirked in a grin that was far too sexy for its own good. "I have to admit, I'm dying for another chance to check out that magnificent chest. Don't make me wait any longer. Because the glimpse I got last night was way too brief."

Arousal punched him in the chest and sunk lower.

"What do you say?" she added, still going full steam ahead with the sexy charm offensive. "You go wash up, I'll make the sandwiches, and then we'll take off in the pickup. Find the perfect spot. We can have a picnic once it's done. Then you can stop worrying about it because it will be over and done."

"I'm not worried about it."

"Prove it," she shot back.

He swore softly, feeling as if he'd been penned in better than the cows that Mystic and he had been herding that morning.

"Fine, dammit. Let's do it. If it'll shut you up."

A triumphant smile lit her face as she did a zipping motion over her mouth. "Consider my lips officially zipped."

Chapter Ten

"LOGAN, RELAX." CHARLIE sighed as she lowered her camera. "I'm shooting you with a Leica not an AK-47."

"I reckon I'd prefer to get shot for real," Logan said, digging his fists into the front pockets of his jeans.

He looked glorious, even with all the pissed-off vibes pumping off him, his muscular shoulders bunched up by his rigid stance. The backdrop of sagebrush and mountain sorrel, and the old-style fence posts that stretched into the distance made the composition breathtaking. Although, not as breathtaking as the man.

But Charlie didn't want this shoot to be too excruciating for him. Getting him to relax though had proved impossible. From the way he was hunching, she knew what the cause was—the burn mark on his chest. The burn mark he was so self-conscious about.

The burn mark that she'd realized as soon as she'd spotted it had been made with the Double T branding iron, because she'd seen the same mark on the cattle. Perhaps it was time to start addressing the real issue here, instead of trying and failing to calm him down with lame jokes.

She lifted the camera back to her face, focused in on Logan's bowed head. "How did you get the scar?"

His expression was shadowed by the cowboy hat he'd plunked on his head as soon as he'd taken off his shirt, but she saw the subtle tension in his abs go rigid. "It was an accident."

"Someone accidentally branded you?" she fired back, still shooting. "How the heck did that happen?"

His head shot up and she saw the flash of blind panic and shame before he had a chance to mask it.

She lowered the camera, her stomach dropping to her toes. "Shit, Logan, it wasn't an accident was it? Someone did that to you on purpose?"

Something hideous had happened to him, something really hideous—and she'd as good as made a joke about it. "I'm so sorry."

He stared up at the snow-capped peaks of the mountain, his lips clamped shut. Even though she knew she was stepping over all kinds of boundaries, she didn't think, she just reacted.

Slinging the camera over her shoulder, she walked toward him. "Who was it, Logan?"

His chin dropped to his chest, his shoulders slumping as all the air left his lungs. "He was drunk at the time; he didn't know what he was doing." He shrugged, the movement somehow so hopeless it made Charlie's heart hurt. "He started drinking when Mom died and he just never stopped."

His father? His father did that to him? How could he?

Everything inside Charlie gathered and without pausing to debate all the reasons why she shouldn't care about this man's pain, because they were just casual bonk buddies, she lifted her arms around Logan's neck and pressed her lips to the scar. She felt the shudder of reaction chase through his body.

She rested her cheek against his bare chest, sunk her fingers into the hair at his nape, and let the single tear spill over her lid before lifting her face to his.

She could see the stunned disbelief in those pure blue eyes. Before he cradled her cheeks.

"Hey, Charlotte, why are you crying?" he said, his voice hoarse, as if he really didn't get it.

"I'm crying for you. Your father shouldn't have done that to you."

He frowned. "It was a long time ago. I'm over it now."

But how could he be, if he was still so ashamed of something that had never been his fault?

She knew Logan was a proud man, that he wouldn't welcome her pity, so she let her anger kick in. "I don't care if you're over it," she said, even though she knew he wasn't really. Because how could you ever get over that kind of abuse?

For goodness' sake, she still hadn't been able to get over her own issues with her mum and dad. The way they'd never

HEIDI RICE

been that interested in her and Em growing up, because they had been selfish, self-absorbed people with unlimited funds who couldn't be bothered to look after their own children, when there were so many other more exciting things they could be doing.

But how much worse would it be to be the child of a man who didn't just ignore or patronize you? A man who would hold his child down and burn his flesh because he'd taken the easy way out and lost himself in a bottle?

"It's no excuse that he was drunk when he did this to you, Logan."

"He didn't know what he was doing. He'd forgotten about it the next day," Logan said, defending a man who didn't deserve to be defended.

"Had he?" she said. "Or had he just decided that he wasn't going to take responsibility for what he'd done?"

"Shit, I guess. I don't know. The drink made him mean. He didn't used to be like that... Not before..." He paused, but the sadness in his voice, the emotion vibrating through him, had another tear slipping over her lid.

Not before Logan's mother died.

She could feel his loneliness and she understood it, because on some level she'd always been lonely too. Even with Em there throughout her childhood, supporting her, telling her that it didn't matter if Daddy and Mummy couldn't come to their birthday again. They had each other, didn't they.

Em had never understood Charlie's anger. Never been able to relate to how furious Charlie had begun to feel when her parents didn't show for another birthday, or another school concert, or another Christmas morning—because they were too busy in Antibes hosting a beach house party for their equally feckless trust-fund friends, or waltzing down the red carpet in Cannes and going to all the after parties. Or skiing in Klosters with the minor royals they were cultivating.

Em had slipped so easily into the role of good girl, trying so hard to make her parents notice her on merit, while Charlie had been the bad girl, getting into scrape after scrape—but neither of them had ever been able to cause so much as a ripple in their parents' glittering social schedule, because Justin and Camilla Foster had never been capable of giving a shit about anyone but themselves.

"You know what, Logan—I hate your bloody dad…" She doubted that was the only time the man had hurt his son. "I wish I could get that bloody branding iron and stamp it on him. The bastard."

★

LOGAN HAD THE weirdest urge to laugh, not just at Charlotte's ferocious expression, but also the way it made him feel. And he had no idea why.

Fact was, he didn't even know why he'd blurted out the

truth.

He'd never told anyone about the brand on his chest and how he'd really got it, not even Lyle, especially not Lyle. He'd spent the early days after it had happened sticking with the story that the nasty scab was an accident, an accident he'd inflicted on himself, and then over the years found endless ways to cover it up or deflect attention from it.

But there had been something about standing bare-chested in a damn field without even a scattering of chest hair to disguise the scar, the oil Charlotte had slapped on him burning off in the mid-morning spring sunshine, that had dried up all those old lies and excuses and prevarications and had the whole sad, sordid little story blurting out of him as if he'd just been injected with truth serum.

His humiliation had been complete. But instead of the pity, or the derision he'd expected from her—because what woman wouldn't think a guy was pretty lame if he'd once let his own father brand him like a prize heifer—instead she'd looked fierce and protective, her face full of a kind of strident compassion that for the first time in his life made him feel more than, instead of less than.

And then that single tear had seeped out and glided down her cheek and he'd been poleaxed.

Because he'd bet his last five bucks Charlotte Foster wasn't the kind of woman who ever cried. And now she was crying for him. Or crying for the little kid he'd been back then. Scared and alone and with not one person to turn to whom he could trust now his mommy was no longer there to hold him and stroke his hair and whisper in his ear whenever he had a nightmare: *"Don't you fuss, my serious boy. Mommy's here to keep you safe."*

For so many years the nightmares had been real. And he'd dealt with them the only way he knew how. By taking the licks from his father and keeping the truth from Lyle— because Logan was the only one left to keep his kid brother safe now their mommy was gone. He'd never gotten mad with his old man; all he'd been was scared and anxious and hopeless. Would he be strong enough, good enough, smart enough to keep it all together? But having Charlotte stand up for him, a woman he barely knew, felt kind of awesome. Because it wasn't as if she was standing up for him—Logan Tate aka Deputy Hard-Ass—the guy who had banged her into unconsciousness the night before. No, she was standing up for that scared little kid.

Just thinking about that, and being able to make that separation—between who he was now and who he'd been then—had all the grief and guilt and shame that had been a part of his life for so long lifting off his shoulders. It was a weight he hadn't even realized he'd been carrying all these years. A weight that had worn him down and closed him off. A weight that had prevented him giving that scared little kid a break.

Holding her face, he brushed one of those precious tears away with his thumb. "I reckon we should probably stop talking about this, or I'm going to end up freezing my nipples off before we're done."

Charlotte stepped back and brushed the last tear away with her fist. "True dat," she said, around a watery laugh—as if she'd only just realized how emotional she had become. On his behalf.

"Okay, big guy, let's finish up so we can have our picnic. I'm famished."

She circled him again with her camera, stroking her hand over his shoulder to shift him into the light. Tugging on his hat to bring the brim down over his face.

The touch of her fingers had the familiar hunger burning through him. But he did as he was told, holding the poses that had made him so damn self-conscious a moment ago, but didn't make him feel exposed anymore.

While she snapped off the last of the shots, the concentration on her face as she focused and refocused the camera lens was almost as sexy as seeing her naked draped over his kitchen table. He tried to stay focused on the here and the now, and not the heat humming in his abdomen.

He didn't fight the connection anymore though.

His childhood had been tough, after his mother had died. And the toughest part of all had been keeping it a secret.

But Charlotte had figured out his big secret in a matter of minutes. A secret no one else had ever even bothered to look for, not even Lyle.

And once she'd figured it out, she had stepped right up to the plate without a second thought to defend the boy he'd been—which told him something.

Charlotte had a lot more depth than she wanted to let on.

If she didn't, she wouldn't have been able to connect so easily with the scared little fella that still lurked inside him and whom he'd tried to ignore for so long.

As they settled in the truck and Charlotte unwrapped the wax paper on the sandwiches she'd made earlier, he couldn't help studying that smart, sexy, tough-girl face and wondering if Charlotte had a scared little kid lurking inside her too.

"There you go," she said, handing him a ham and cheese sandwich almost as big as her head. "Try not to dislocate your jaw. These things could double as doorstops. I think I overdid the filling."

He chewed off a chunk, not easy when the size of the thing meant it barely fitted into his mouth, but the perfect combo of salty ham, creamy cheese, and tart mustard and rich mayo had him humming in his throat.

Her eyes flashed to his, the smile knowing before her gaze darted away again.

The zap of awareness sizzled across his nerve endings.

So the photo shoot had turned Charlotte on too. Good to know.

"You want a pickle?" she said, rummaging around in the bag she'd stuffed the sandwiches into.

"Sure."

She handed him one and then plopped a serviette on his lap.

She bent down to reach beneath the bench seat, then straightened, producing the flask he used on overnight trail rides.

"Ta-dah," she said, grinning as she unscrewed the cap. "I also have fresh coffee. Never let it be said that Charlie Foster doesn't know how to pack the perfect picnic." She whipped two metal mugs out of her bag of all things and perched them on the dash to pour them each a cup of coffee. The steaming aroma filled the cab, but did nothing to mask that sultry scent that had been driving him wild for a while now.

"I hope you're okay with black?" she said, picking up her own cup to blow on it. "I couldn't find anything to put the cream in without it ending up all over our paving-slab sandwiches."

He laughed around another mouthful of ham and cheese, then gulped down some hot coffee before he choked.

Why did he get the weirdest feeling she was nervous? She'd always been a talkative type of woman, but all her usual snark seemed to have disappeared as they stood out in the top pasture and she took her pictures. Without that edge, there was something about the motor-mouthed commentary on their picnic that he found really endearing. A side to her that was younger, more innocent, and as captivating as the rest of her—like he was getting a glimpse of Charlotte without her armor.

He dumped his sandwich on his lap, and took a bite of pickle, contemplating his next move. Maybe it wasn't his business, but hell, she'd jumped right into his business this afternoon and the result had been...okay... So he didn't see why he shouldn't satisfy at least some of his curiosity about her.

"What about your folks, Charlotte? Do you have any?"

She glanced his way, then shrugged, the movement deliberately casual.

So casual it broke his heart when she said: "Not anymore. They died in a plane crash when Em and I were eighteen."

"Damn, I'm sorry. That sucks." She'd been orphaned too, at a young age. Maybe not as young as him and Lyle when they'd lost their mom, but still young enough to have it hurt pretty bad.

But instead of accepting his condolences, her voice remained flat and indifferent. "Don't be. We weren't close."

"No?" he delved.

She slanted him an exasperated look. "Okay, is this the moment when I tell you about my shitty childhood to let you off the hook?"

"What?" he said, because she'd lost him there.

"You had a really shitty childhood, Logan. Mine wasn't half as shitty. So you don't have to feel bad for me in return."

"Then you won't feel weird about telling me why you weren't close with your folks?" he said, not letting her hide behind her usual snark.

He knew a distraction technique when he saw one.

"Oh for…" She plopped her own sandwich down. Had the subject of her parents ruined her appetite? "Fine, do you want the full sob story, or just the abridged version?"

"The full story."

She gave a theatrical sigh. "Okay, once upon a time there were two poor little rich girls." She sent him her best mocking smile, the one he now knew she used to avoid serious conversations. "Their parents were wealthy London socialites. Their father had a family connection to one of the Queen's ladies in waiting, which he milked mercilessly. And their mother was the only daughter of a hedge-fund manager and his trophy wife. Camilla and Justin were both trust-fund babies who spent all their time chasing the next great party or soiree or event. They traveled widely—always in First Class. Made it their mission to throw the most talked-about event of the season every year. Loved each other with one of those grand passions only reserved for the spoilt and immature. And did not have the first clue what to do with unplanned twin daughters once their children had grown out of the cute-baby-photo-op phase and started to talk back."

She chugged down a mouthful of the hot coffee and he watched her throat bob. Had to be thirsty work keeping up the pretense of not giving a damn about something that must have hurt like hell when you were a kid. "By the time Em and I were four we had begun to totally cramp their style. So they washed their hands of us. Stuck us in boarding schools year-round, hired a governess and a housekeeper for those pesky school holidays, and visited us maybe once or twice a year like we were exotic animals in a zoo. Then one day—the day after mine and Em's eighteenth birthday, which of course they'd been far too busy to attend—the housekeeper gave us the news the private plane they were traveling in went down over the Swiss Alps. Bummer really, because apparently there was some great snow in Klosters that year and they missed it."

The flippant remark couldn't hide the bite of bitterness—or the well of pain beneath.

Logan placed his hand over the ones Charlotte had clasped in her lap, and brushed his thumb over the whitened knuckles. So that was where the spooky connection he'd felt came from. She knew too, exactly what it felt like to be less than. To people who should have cared about you.

Lifting her stiff fingers, he kissed her palm. "It still sucks."

She curled her fingers closed, the quirk of her lips more confused than amused. "I suppose."

"So you've got a twin sister?" he said, eager to know more—and keen to change the subject, because for a moment there she had looked so vulnerable. He didn't want to think about that tough little girl trying and failing to get her parents' attention.

"Yes. We're identical twins."

"No kidding?" He chuckled. "How the heck has the world survived with two of you roaming around?"

Charlotte smiled, the cheeky grin captivating him more. "Because we're only identical in theory," she said. "Emily is the smart, sensible, good twin. I got all the bad twin genes. Just ask our head teachers."

"Head teachers? Plural?"

She laughed and nodded. "Uh-huh, I managed to get expelled from..." She paused as if considering the number—the glint in her eye suggesting this was an achievement to be proud of. "I think it was five different boarding schools by the time I'd graduated. Poor old Em got dragged out with me because she refused to stay any place I wasn't welcome. Em's not only smart and sensible, she's also super loyal."

"I'd like to meet her one day," he said.

Charlotte tugged her hand out of his. "Unlikely," she said. "Em doesn't travel well. And I don't generally introduce her to my hookups."

Were they still just a hookup? The thought irritated him for no good reason. But he didn't say anything. He'd figured something out about Charlotte today. Something she would probably hate for him to know.

She wasn't half as tough as she pretended to be.

"Speaking of which..." She placed her sandwich on the dash. Then lifted his coffee cup out of his hand before placing that on the dash too... "When's the last time you had a shag in a pickup truck?" she said.

"A shag?" he said, enjoying the dumb British word. Heat pooled in his groin at the saucy smile as she lifted up and straddled his lap. She planted her palms on his chest, under the shirt he hadn't bothered to button up, and then slid them down his ribs. Sensation leapt and jumped at the firm caress, her fingertips gliding under his waistband, before she set about unbuckling his belt.

"Charlotte?" he said, his hands coming to rest on her butt. "What the hell are you doing?" he added in the sternest voice he could muster while every molecule of blood in his brain was charging south.

The playful smile became more than a bit wicked as she ripped open his fly and pressed her palm against the straining ridge in shorts. "I'd say it's pretty obvious."

"We're out in the open here," he said, not sure why he found the thought so damn arousing. Maybe Lyle wasn't the only exhibitionist in the family.

She glanced around as if checking for people. "So what? There's no one about." Her finger trailed under his shorts, and fondled his erection.

He groaned and jerked against her touch. The little tease.

"Unbutton my shirt, Logan," she said. "I want to feel those big, callused hands of yours on my tits."

This was just another distraction technique. He knew it. But his mind was already way too far down in his pants to think clearly. The brush of her knuckles tortured him as she released the erection and wrapped her fingers around the turgid length.

He sucked in a breath as she began to stroke him in smooth even strokes.

He did as he was told, unbuttoning her shirt and then pulling it down until it hung from her shoulders.

He traced the purple lace edge of her bra, then delved beneath to pull one ripe breast out. He licked at the nipple, gratified when she bucked and set off the car horn.

"Bugger," she said, as he laughed.

Settling back down, she continued to stroke him, while he placed his lips on her nipple, drew the succulent peak into his mouth.

She sighed. "Has anyone ever told you, Logan, you have the most magnificent cock?" The confidence in her tone was almost as compelling as the play of her thumb over the head of his penis.

"Not lately," he managed, as he blew on the wet nipple, then released her other breast from its lacy confinement.

The battle continued as she stroked and caressed and he sucked and licked.

"Oh God, I want you inside me," she murmured, bowing back, thrusting her breasts into his mouth.

He pulled back, his dick ready to explode. Grasping her hand, he dragged it off his cock.

"Get out of your damn pants," he said, his voice gruff

with desperation.

She swore, then scrambled around, but the space was too cramped with her on his lap. Grasping her round the waist, he lifted her off him, and dumped her on the seat of the cab.

His elbow knocked the steering wheel; her head thudded against the opposite door as he grabbed her boots and tugged them off. Then he undid her jeans and dragged them down her hips with her wiggling furiously to help him.

He swore. "Next time we decide to do this, could you wear a damn skirt?"

"Absolutely," she said, breathing heavily, as he managed to yank the confining denim past her knees. "As soon as it's not cold enough to freeze my fanny off, I am going to be wearing skirts with no undies."

He laughed as he flung the jeans over the seat, then yanked her panties down and off. "Glad to hear it."

Lifting her knees until she was open for him, he thrust deep.

The vicious climax licked at the base of his spine, her breasts jiggling in front of him, propped up by the bra he hadn't bothered to take off.

Bracing her hands against the door, she sobbed, the sound low and deep, spurring him on, spurring him up.

His knee was jammed against the seat, his boots ramming the door. The whole cab rocked on its springs, the thump thump thump of the suspension matched her gasps of breath and his grunts. Steam gathered on the windshield cocooning them from the outside world.

She grasped his buttocks in greedy hands, demanding he go deeper, take more. His lips found the pulse point in her neck. She cried out as her climax hit. Her muscles spasmed, gripping his aching cock and massaging the whole length.

Not yet, not yet. Fuck now…

He dragged himself out, pumping his spurting seed against the soft skin of her belly as the orgasm roared through him like a freight train.

He collapsed on top of her, the cab finally bouncing to a stop. His galloping heartbeat finally slowed to a canter.

It took him a while to come back to reality. To realize he was in the cab of his truck and he'd just screwed Charlotte into the upholstery.

The air stank of sex and her, the wild coupling just about the most nuts he'd ever had. His elbow hurt like a son of a bitch, and he had his pants down round his damn ankles, his naked butt chilled by the spring air. But the pheromones still firing through his bloodstream made him feel invincible.

Lifting up he rolled off her. And sat up.

"That was nuts," he said as he began scooting his jeans up over his hips.

"Nuts but fun," she said.

"Yeah."

She looked as satisfied as he felt, but then a warm light came into her eyes. Her expression still hot, but also somehow tender. His heartbeat cantered back up to a gallop.

"Guess what? That was a first for me," she announced, looking pretty damn pleased with herself. She pushed her unruly hair behind her ears. "I've never done it in a vehicle before."

"Me either."

"Really?" Her head tilted to one side. "I thought all American teenagers made out in their parents' cars. Now I'm disappointed."

"They do, generally."

"Then why didn't you?" she said. "And don't tell me it's 'cos you didn't have a girlfriend who would let you get in her panties. Because I don't believe you. No girl would be able to resist that magnificent cock."

He laughed. *Holy crap, did the woman have no shame at all?*

"I had a couple of girlfriends. Never got past second base with either one of them. I never had the time to treat them right. While the other guys were busy making out on the River Road after football practice I was always at the ranch, looking out for Lyle or doing the heavy chores he was too little to do." Or his old man was too drunk to do. "And when Pop died I had to quit school altogether." Because there had been no one else to take on the responsibility.

He concentrated on re-buttoning his fly, while she leaned over the seat to retrieve her jeans and the boots he'd chucked into the back of the cab.

"How boring for you," she said, bouncing back down

next to him.

"Yeah. It was kind of dull." Funny, he'd never thought about that until now. How much he'd missed out on as a teenager because of all the stuff he had to look after.

"Well, it's a good thing I'm here to show you what you've been missing," she said.

"Ain't that the truth," he said and grinned, captivated all over again by her wild streak. Maybe it was just the endorphins talking—which were still charging through his bloodstream like thoroughbreds heading for the finish line at the Kentucky Derby—but somehow he didn't think so.

Charlotte was right. He'd always been super safe and responsible as a kid—not just about sex but about every part of his life. Because he'd known there wasn't anyone to catch him if he fell.

But suddenly the thought of what they could be doing together while Charlotte was at the Double T charged through his head.

Charlotte's wildness brought something rich and vivid into his life that he hadn't even realized was missing until now. For once in his life he didn't have to give a damn about what people thought or what had to be done next; he could just wallow in how good having her around made him feel.

It wouldn't last. Heck, Charlotte would probably drive him over the edge if she stayed for much longer than a couple of weeks—because generally he preferred his life to be steady and predictable. And she'd no doubt get bored with him.

But right this minute, with his body still humming from the adrenaline rush of hot sweaty, pickup truck sex, he felt like a teenager, drunk on lust and endorphins and possibilities. The teenager he'd never been allowed to be when he was a teenager.

"Oh. My. God." She said as if she'd just discovered the secret of life. "You know what this means, Logan?"

"What?"

The teasing glint in her eyes made him smile.

"We just christened your truck," she declared.

"We sure did." The grin split his face as she laughed— that rich smoky seductive laugh that he was fast becoming addicted to.

He turned on the ignition—and began chuckling with her as they bounced down the dirt track that led off the high pasture.

They carried on laughing together across the pastureland and over the creek road until they reached the ranch.

He felt like a naughty kid who had gotten away with something. And Charlotte was his partner in crime.

She jumped down from the truck, having gathered up the picnic stuff. Lifting her camera bag off the seat, she slung it over her shoulder.

"I need a shower. To wash all your little swimmers off my stomach," she said, outrageous as ever. "Then I'm going to upload the shots from today."

"You want me to cook supper later?" he asked, already imagining what they could get up to on the kitchen table for dessert.

"Sure," she said. "I should have some contacts to show you by then." She bounced up on tiptoes, grabbed his cheeks, and planted a quick kiss on his lips. "Thanks for a great afternoon, Logan," she finished, before letting him go and skipping up the porch steps to disappear into the house.

He couldn't wipe the dumb grin off his face as he watched the screen door slam.

But it wasn't until he'd saddled up Mystic and was riding the colt to the calving pens to help Tad and Ryan feed and water the pregnant cows, that he realized he'd begun to whistle.

Chapter Eleven

C HARLIE SET THE timer in the glow of infrared light and switched on the enlarger. The negative image of Logan's head and torso that she had taken over a week ago in the high pasture imprinted itself onto the eight by ten rectangle of photographic paper. The enlarger clicked off and she lifted the paper with her thumb and forefinger, set the timer to one minute, and dropped the print into the tray of developer.

She held her breath while she swished the fluid backward and forward as the image gradually came to life.

This was where the magic happened.

Logan appeared, his eyes downcast, his jaw strong, his chest solid, his expression resolute. The white fencing behind him created a stark line against the varying grays of the sagebrush in the pasture. And the monolith of Copper Mountain in the background. But it was the monolith of the man himself that grabbed all the attention. And made Charlie's breath catch.

The man who she'd discovered so much more about than when this picture was taken. And yet seemed to know and understand even less.

The past week had gone by in a blur of insanely hot sex, and so many moments of humor, teasing and, most seductive of all, companionship. And while that touched her on so many levels, it terrified her on others.

Logan Tate was not the man she had once assumed he was. Nor was he the man he had become that day on the hill pasture. He was so much more than that. She wasn't sure she'd ever met a man who was as steady and loyal and logical as he was. As strong and dependable and determined. But neither had she met a man who also had so many hidden depths. So many different layers and complexities.

She'd thought he was the polar opposite of her—in personality and in his whole outlook on life. She'd believed that despite the incendiary physical connection between them, Logan was far too settled and confident and assured to ever hold her attention for more than a few days. But it had been ten days now since they'd started sleeping together, and every single thing she'd discovered about him had blurred each of those certainties. He captivated her. Not just that rugged handsome face, all his hot moves in bed and that magnificent cock, but his humor, his openness, and his generosity of spirit.

For the first time ever, she had no desire to move on. Or not yet. Which was unusual in itself. Ever since she'd left London age eighteen, she'd never spent more than a week, two at the most, in the same spot—she'd always been itching to move on in a matter of days.

Not so now. If anything she was already contemplating the end of the project, and knowing a month would not be long enough to satisfy her curiosity about the man whose bed she shared.

And yup, she'd actually begun sleeping in Logan's bed and not just jumping him there. Another first for her, because while she'd had boyfriends and lots of them, she had always rebelled against the thought of having a man invade her personal space. For that reason she'd been reluctant when Logan had first suggested she move into his room for the duration. But once Lyle had returned from his smoke jumper training, and any more epic shags on the kitchen table had been out, moving into Logan's room had made sense.

Even so, she had assumed she'd want to tiptoe back into her own bed after they'd made love. But somehow, the first night after Lyle's return, Logan had tucked her against his chest and she'd drifted into a dreamless sleep so deep the next thing she'd been aware of was waking up to the sound of birdsong with Logan's impressive morning erection pressing into her buttocks.

The man had turned her into a stealth snuggler, for chrissake. As well as a nymphomaniac. And while she could live with the nymphomania, she wasn't sure about the snuggling.

She'd never done intimacy before in relationships. Not with any of the other guys she'd dated. But with Logan it had just happened. He'd told her about his father, about the abuse he'd suffered, and the challenges he'd faced and overcome, and she'd felt connected to him on some weird subliminal level.

So much so, that when he'd asked she'd blurted out all the crap about her own parents. But instead of seeing what she'd wanted him to see—that she was tough and invulnerable—she had the terrifying suspicion he'd seen exactly the opposite. The sad little rich girl who had spent her whole childhood yearning to be hugged, accepted, appreciated, yearning to be told she mattered. Then he had gone one step further and found a way to fill that need without her ever having to ask.

And now she was bloody addicted not just to the sex, but to the moments afterward, when he would wrap his arms around her and she'd feel safer and more secure than she'd ever felt before in her life. Logan Tate made her feel special, important, cherished.

Which was of course bonkers, because they hardly knew each other—and she didn't yearn to feel cherished or special anyway.

Get real, Charlie. This is simply the epic sex talking; that's what you're really addicted to.

But if sex with Logan was all she was addicted to, why did everything else about him, and all the things they'd done together in the last ten days—that didn't involve getting naked—feel so important?

The evening spent watching Lyle play guitar at Flint-Works, when Logan had tried and resolutely failed to teach her the Texas two-step. All the meals they'd shared together while chatting about their different activities during the day. And worst of all the horse rides they'd taken over Double T land, through the pine forest one frosty morning, or into the foothills of Copper Mountain one afternoon while Logan was roping the last of the pregnant cattle to bring them down to the calving pens.

As if the way Logan could make her body feel wasn't bad enough, she had developed an addiction to his company and even to the land itself. Montana's wide-open spaces, its rich palette of greens, blues, and golds, and the breathtaking vistas he'd introduced her to on the Double T had left her spellbound.

Even the authentic rhythm of life on the ranch had seduced her. And being with Logan, seeing how he fit not just into the wild untamed landscape but also the settled secure life in the ranch house, had only seduced her more.

She knew in her heart, that just like the man, she could photograph his home for the rest of her days without ever uncovering all its secrets.

She lifted the print out of the developer as the timer clicked off, then slipped it into the stop tray—to prevent the image becoming overdeveloped—and reset the timer for another minute.

Even in the ruddy infrared glow she could make out the

strong lines of Logan's face and body, the disks of his nipples, the shadows cast over his expression by the cowboy hat he had tipped over his forehead… And the dark mark of the scar over his left breast.

She'd already prepared and catalogued a series of digital color shots from the shoot and, as she'd promised him, had worked in Photoshop to eliminate the scar. But as she tilted the tray to fix the black-and-white image, her breathing slowed.

This was the image she wanted to use. Stark, simple, and effortlessly seductive.

Because what Logan thought of as an imperfection, an ugly reminder of his childhood, to her represented his strength and compassion—and all the things about his personality that showed the strong, beautiful man who had risen like a phoenix out of the ashes of that abused child.

They hadn't talked about their pasts since that afternoon, but the more time she spent with Logan, the more she watched him interact with Lyle and the other ranch hands and the folks in Marietta and even with her, she could see that streak of goodness and strength that went so much deeper than his rugged good looks or his insane sex appeal.

Logan Tate was a keeper.

She plucked the image out of the fixer with her tongs, and switched on the main bathroom light. She dropped the print into the pool of running water in the bathroom sink and pulled out one of the earlier prints that had been rinsing long enough.

As she pinned the other shot of Logan—his eyes focused on her—to the line she'd strung across the room, the wave of melancholy overwhelmed her.

One day some other woman would hook Logan, would fall in love with him and make babies with him and take his mother's place as the mistress of the Double T.

But that woman could never be her, because unlike Logan, she had never had any staying power.

Maybe right now she didn't want to leave the Double T, was anxious at the prospect of having to leave Logan and Marietta once the project was done, because she'd become addicted to the pace of life here and the time she spent in his arms. But eventually the wanderlust would return—most likely just when she'd convinced herself she could stick, that she wanted to stick. And once that happened she'd feel trapped again. The way she had in boarding school, or after her parents' funeral.

She just didn't do commitment and trust. She didn't consider it a weakness; it just wasn't who she was. Or could ever be. However much of a stealth snuggler she'd become.

At the moment she was enjoying discovering all the many facets and layers and complexities of Logan Tate—and reveling in the physical pleasures of having insanely hot sex with him—but eventually she would have to pull herself back from the edge.

Or risk falling right off a cliff—into an uncharted land

that had all but destroyed her sense of self and self-worth as a child. The problem was figuring out when to pull back. And how. Before it was too late.

The thump on the door made her jump. "Dammit, Charlotte, have you been washed down the goddamn drain? You've been in there for hours. It's close to midnight."

She wrenched open the door, to find Logan on the other side wearing nothing but a pair of pajama bottoms and a scowl.

"I told you not to wait up for me," she said, even if her heart did a little jump and skip at the concern shadowing those deep blue eyes.

When exactly had she become one of Logan's responsibilities? And how did she feel about it? Not as irritated as she should was the answer—if her jumping, jiving heartbeat was anything to go by.

He thrust his hand through his hair. "And I told you I can't sleep knowing you're busy developing pictures of other guys naked while you should be in bed with me."

Her answering smile was quick and entirely inappropriate. She didn't like possessive guys any more than she appreciated overprotective ones. When exactly had it become so cute on Logan?

"What the heck are you smiling about?" he said, going the full grumpy. "I've got to be up at five tomorrow to head up to Copper Ridge with Tad and fix some fencing. Give me a damn break, okay, and come to bed."

"Would it make you feel better if you knew I wasn't developing shots of other guys?"

"Huh?"

She pushed open the bathroom door and ushered him inside. "Take a look for yourself. They're all of you, Othello."

He wandered into the small room, immediately sucking most of the spare oxygen out of it. The slopes and muscles of his back, and those low-riding PJ pants kicked off the inevitable melting sensation in her abdomen.

She turned off the faucet and lifted her final print out of the sink. After flicking off the excess water, she pinned it to her drying line while he studied the shots already there.

Awareness rippled through her and she rubbed the back of her neck—maybe it was time to call it a night and get more of what Logan had to offer in bed—and stop panicking about what the future would hold. Because they had no future. And that had always been understood.

Her obsession with Logan was primarily sexual. Anything else was just the inevitable fallout of how invested in this project she had become. She was getting worried about nothing. Her wanderlust would return as soon as the project was over.

And Logan was such a guarded, moody bugger, she didn't need to worry about him falling in love with her. Any more than she needed to worry about her falling in love with him. They'd been living in a false reality the past ten days, spending way too much time in each other's company.

She didn't belong on the Double T any more than Logan could function off it.

But then he reached up to pluck the photo she had just pinned off the line and bent his head down to examine it.

She slid her hands around his midriff, unable to resist touching that firm flesh a moment longer, and pressed her cheek to the muscles of his spine. Maybe he wouldn't belong to her forever, but he belonged to her right now.

"What do you think?" she asked, when he stayed silent, the harsh thuds of his heartbeat reverberating against her cheek.

It shouldn't matter what he thought of the shot, but somehow it did.

"You made it look…" He hesitated, taking a deep breath that made his ribs expand under her arms. "You made the scar look okay," he finished, as if he couldn't believe it. "How did you do that?"

"It doesn't just look okay," she said. "It looks heroic. And it looks that way, because it is," she said, saddened that he found that so hard to believe.

He twisted round, forcing her to let go of him, the intensity in his eyes burning right through the tough shield she had always kept around her emotions to the tender spot that still ached for the little boy he'd once been.

"How can it be heroic?" he said, his voice hoarse with confusion. "I let him do that to me. It's humiliating, not heroic."

"Oh, Logan," she said. "Can't you see? You had a choice. You could have run away." The way she would have. "Or you could have told everyone what was going on, but you didn't. You stayed to protect Lyle, and you kept it secret to protect everyone… Even the man who hurt you. To protect everyone except yourself. If you can't see how heroic that is, then you're an idiot."

★

EMOTION SLAMMED INTO Logan, closing his throat.

What the hell did he do with this woman? This woman who made him feel so much more than he had ever felt? This woman who was all wrong for him but felt so right?

After pinning the single shot back up onto her line, he sunk his hands into her hair, and plundered her mouth. He let the hunger storm through him, in the blind hope that it would obliterate the yearning.

Wanting anyone this much was never good, but wanting a woman like Charlotte? Wild, mercurial, passionate, and unpredictable Charlotte? That was a recipe for disaster.

He'd loved a woman once with every fiber of his being— his mother. And then he'd lost her—because his love hadn't been enough. He couldn't let himself love and need someone that much again. Especially someone he knew he would never be able to hold.

But he was finding it harder and harder to resist the pull inside him that got stronger and more insistent each day. The pull to declare his feelings.

The sex was incredible. So hot and raw and exciting. But much more disturbing were these moments—when she opened herself up to him. When she showed him the compassionate, brave, and generous side of her character that he was pretty sure she kept hidden from everyone else behind her tough-girl exterior. And it was destroying his will to resist her, and resist the strength of his own feelings.

Threading her fingers into his hair, she plundered his mouth right back, responding with the honesty and hunger he had come to adore.

He drew away first, and boosted her slim body easily into his arms.

"You about finished here?" he said, struggling to lift the mood. Struggling to focus on the hunger firing through his bloodstream and not the erratic rhythm of his heart. "Because I'm more than ready to screw you into unconsciousness so I can finally get some sleep tonight."

She laughed, the gleam of mischief in her eye as captivating as her impassioned defense of him a moment ago.

"You're on, Deputy Hard-Ass," she said, grasping his shoulders as he toted her out of the tiny bathroom.

She peppered butterfly kisses along his jaw, which only inflamed the hunger. "But don't be surprised if I screw you into unconsciousness first."

He chuckled as he headed up the stairs, the swell of heat in his crotch making his erection butt against the warm cleft between her legs—but as he dropped her onto his bed and began to tear off her clothes, he'd never felt less amused in his life.

As he plunged into the tight wet heat, and rocked them both to another vicious climax, he could feel himself falling headfirst into a pit of trouble.

With no idea whatsoever if he would survive the landing.

Chapter Twelve

CHARLIE WAVED RYAN goodbye as he drove off toward the bunkhouse, and then she walked into the ranch, her boots crunching on the frosty grass. The screen door cracked behind her, and ricocheted off the headache she'd been brewing all day. She'd spent the drive back to the ranch on her mobile phone busy schmoozing an old friend, who was one of the commissioning editors at *Vanity Fair*, into doing a feature on the calendar.

Now all she had to do was get the release forms signed for the shots they were interested in using—and schedule the last shoot.

She dragged off her coat and placed it on the coat hooks in the hallway, then dug her phone back out of the pocket while she kicked off her boots.

She typed out yet another text to Jonah Clark, the subject of her last shoot, a thirty-two-year-old search-and-rescue pilot who had proved more bloody elusive than the Loch Ness Monster.

She pressed send and deposited her camera in the darkroom. Not expecting a prompt reply. Didn't matter, she might not even be here to do the shoot.

Anxiety made her stomach tighten as she stuffed the pharmacy bag she'd had hidden in her camera bag into her tote. Working on the project had helped take her mind off the problem she had finally acknowledged this morning, when she'd spotted the bright red P on her phone calendar and realized her period was now late by over a week.

She'd never been particularly regular, but a whole week? She and Logan had been careful, using condoms every time they'd made love. All except one time. That one time when they'd christened his pickup truck after his photo shoot.

When she hadn't been working on the project today she'd been frantically looking up 'methods of contraception' on the Internet and discovered that withdrawal was just about the most unreliable, short of using no contraception at all.

She heard shouting coming from the living room and the backchat of TV sports commentary.

Standing in the doorway in her stocking feet, she watched Logan and Lyle unobserved as they argued about the chances of the Minnesota Wild coming back against the Chicago Blackhawks.

The anxiety in her stomach twisted tighter. What would she do if she was pregnant?

Don't think about that. Not yet. Not until you know.

She'd read the instructions in the box three times after buying it that afternoon in town—and knew that to get an accurate result she had to wait until tomorrow morning to pee on the stick.

She couldn't tell Logan. She had no idea how he would react, but until she had peed on the stick this wasn't his problem; it was hers. And if the result came back positive? What then? Did she really want to tell him? What if he wanted her to have the baby? What if he didn't? Did she even know how she felt?

The questions kept crashing into each other in her head. She felt like a rudderless ship, colliding into everything and anything.

Before she'd ever met Logan this would not have been a problem.

She'd certainly never been dumb enough to let any guy get even close to getting her pregnant. But more than that, she had always had a very clear view of herself. Who she was and what she wanted out of life. What she was capable of and what she wasn't.

Motherhood, babies, homes, hearths, love and romance, and all that domestic goddess crap had never been what she was looking for. She was an adrenaline junkie, a free agent, a photographer, a wild child, always looking for the next amazing shot, the next great adventure.

But somewhere, somehow, in the last three weeks of living at the Double T, of living with Logan—in his arms, in his bed—everything had become confused. So confused she didn't even know how she felt about the possibility of being unexpectedly pregnant.

What the hell had Logan done to her? And how did she put it right? Get her sense of self, her sense of certainty back again? Quickly enough to deal with what the pee stick might tell her tomorrow morning?

The pulse of emotion smothered her chest when Logan's head turned—as if he'd sensed her standing there.

"Hey, Charlotte," he said, the smile that spread across those beautiful lips both sexy and pleased to see her. "Come and take a load off. The Wild are about to make their final power play."

He reached out an arm and beckoned her forward.

"They better hurry up," Lyle said, not sounding optimistic. "With only five on the clock and Staal in the box."

Charlie settled onto the worn couch cushions beside Logan, the emotion choking her when he wrapped his arm around her waist—treating her like she belonged, like this wasn't just a temporary relationship. Like they were a real couple. The way he'd treated her right from the start, despite all her efforts to keep the distance she usually did. The distance she had somehow lost along the way. And now couldn't seem to relocate even though she desperately needed it.

"You want a beer?" he said, considerate and kind, the way he always was.

She shook her head. "No thanks."

"Give me a break, you two." Lyle slanted them both an

exasperated look. "If you're going to start necking, I'm out of here."

"Shut up, Lyle," Logan said, a good-humored smirk on his face as he sunk back into the seat and nudged Charlie closer. He made a big production of nuzzling at her neck—she would guess for the benefit of his brother who swore on cue—but the spurt of arousal shot through Charlie regardless.

How come he could still turn her inside out with lust after close to a month of nonstop hot sex?

"Don't, Logan." She pressed her elbow into his ribs.

He released her, but the look he sent her—concerned and way too perceptive—only made the pulsing in her chest become unbearable. "What's up, Charlotte? You look beat."

"Nothing," she said, forcing herself to stand.

She felt the loss of his warmth instantly, which only disturbed her more. If she couldn't even get up from the couch without feeling as if she'd severed a limb, how the hell was she going to walk away from him?

"I've just got a bit of a headache," she murmured. "Anyone thought about supper?" she added, desperate for something to do. Anything to do that didn't involve sinking into Logan's welcoming arms. Or panicking about the testing kit burning a hole in her tote.

"We got pizzas, loaded," Logan said. "We saved you a couple of slices, you want me to nuke 'em for you?" he added, getting ready to get up from the couch.

"I've got it." She waved him back down. "I've got some stuff to sort out." She could organize the release forms for the *Vanity Fair* article on her tablet and eat in the kitchen. And thus contain the urge to blurt out her worries to Logan.

This wasn't his decision, if there was even a decision to make. It was hers. She didn't lean on other people. Didn't need them. She was an island. That was the way she liked it.

She escaped into the kitchen, but as soon as she'd located the saved pizza slices and popped them in the microwave, Logan appeared in the doorway.

"What are you doing?" she snapped. "I can nuke a few pizza slices on my own."

"I know," he said, walking into the room.

"And you've got the big game to watch."

"It's just an exhibition match, not that big a game."

Right, because she knew sod all about ice hockey.

The microwave pinged. She grabbed the steaming slice without thinking and yelped as hot cheese burnt her hand.

Logan was by her side in an instant, with a cold towel to press on the burn. "What was that you were saying about being able to nuke pizza slices on your own?" he said, the humor in his voice gruff and easy.

She tugged her hand free. "Stop it!"

He stared at her—that patient, pensive look unnerving her more. The hint of humor was gone.

"Stop crowding me," she said, even though he wasn't really. "I can't stand it."

"Then stop pretending nothing's wrong. I can see something's bothering you."

She heard the snap in his voice, and realized she wasn't the only frustrated one.

"I told you, I have a headache." Picking up the now cooling pizza she shoved it onto a plate then picked up her tote and slung it over her shoulder. The tote that felt as if it weighed a hundred tons—because so much guilt and confusion was stuffed into the slim cardboard box that sat like a bolder inside it. "I'm going to bed."

My own bed, in my own room.

The room she should have stayed in all along. She'd be able to find the separation she needed right now if she had never moved into Logan's room. Never gotten so wound up in a life that wasn't hers. A life she shouldn't want.

He stared at her, the searching expression one that made the pulsing emotion choke off her air supply.

She was being a bitch. But she couldn't seem to stop herself. She didn't want to hurt him. But how could she not, when she could never be the woman he needed?

She left him standing in the kitchen and stomped up the stairs with her plate of leftover pizza and her ten-ton bag. Arriving in the room she hadn't slept in in over three weeks, she dumped the uneaten pizza on the dresser and lay down on the bed.

The sting of tears came without warning. She shoved her fist into her mouth to stop them falling and curled onto the pillow. But she doubted she'd be able to sleep. Because the rudderless ship in her stomach had turned into the *Titanic* and it was heading straight for an iceberg.

★

"WHAT'S UP WITH Charlie? It her time of the month?" Lyle asked from his seat on the opposite couch as Logan walked back into the room.

"Shut up, Lyle," he said but without heat as he sat back on the couch.

The game had finished and the reporter was going through the play-by-play stats. The Wild had lost. But he didn't give a damn.

He'd wanted to follow her up, wanted to be sure she was okay. Something was wrong. Something was really wrong. It wasn't like her to snap, or scold. He'd seen the anxiety in her eyes. The flash of panic.

He'd been feeling pretty anxious himself in the last few days, the last week. The project was drawing to a close. She hadn't mentioned moving on, and he hadn't brought it up, but he knew—had known for a while—that he didn't want her to leave.

They were good together. And not just in bed. She'd brought light and warmth and laughter into his life in a few short weeks. This place would be cold and dark and lonely again when she was gone—with him and Lyle rattling around the rooms. The house had felt like a home again for the first time in twenty-three years. Like the home it had been before his mom passed.

It sounded sentimental and kind of cheesy but it was the truth.

He couldn't let her leave without telling her he wanted her to stay. He knew that, but he hadn't figured out how to say it yet without freaking her out. And he was running out of time.

And now this. Whatever the heck this was.

His cell phone buzzed and he picked it up off the coffee table.

He saw Betty on the call signal—the station's dispatcher. And took the call. Hoping that it wasn't going to be an emergency. He didn't want to leave the house tonight. Not with Charlotte so out of sorts upstairs.

"Hey, Betty, it's Logan."

"Logan, oh hi, I thought the phone would probably go to voice mail. You not watching the match?"

"It just finished. The Wild lost." He frowned. So it obviously wasn't an emergency, or Betty would have given him the info straight off. And why did she sound so sheepish. "Is there a problem?" he asked, wanting her to get to the point.

"Now don't get all huffy, Logan. I know you don't like me spreading rumors, but I heard something from Carol Bingley in the pharmacy and I thought I should tell you, because…" She paused.

Goddamn. Did she think he was one of the old girls she gossiped with over eggnog and snickerdoodles at Nell's Cut and Curl? "Spit it out, Betty," he said.

"Carol said that pretty young photographer bought a pregnancy test kit this afternoon," Betty blurted out. "And I thought you should know about it. Just in case you didn't."

His heart stopped; it literally stopped beating, then thundered so hard against his ribs he felt like the guy in that old sci-fi movie who had an alien leap right out of his chest.

Holy shit. No wonder Charlie had looked so anxious. And panicked. She thought she might be pregnant? Had she taken the test already? Why hadn't she said anything to him?

"Logan, are you still there?" Betty's voice came down the line, curious and obviously angling for a good story to tell the Golden Girls Gossip Club.

"I already knew about it, Betty," he lied. "But you tell Carol I'll be having words with her next time I'm in Marietta Pharmacy. People's private business is their private business—she shouldn't be spreading that stuff all around town. It isn't ethical."

"Why that's ridiculous, Logan. No need to get all uppity about it with Carol," Betty said, getting uppity. "She only mentioned it to me in passing."

He'd just bet she had. Carol was worse than Betty, between the two of them they could weasel secrets out of Jason Bourne. But he didn't have time to explain the importance of tact and diplomacy to a woman past sixty.

"And you're the only one I've told," Betty added, for once sounding a tiny bit circumspect.

He doubted that, but he said: "Then you need to keep it that way. Charlotte Foster is doing this town a huge favor and I don't want her private business…" *their private business* "…becoming the subject of tittle-tattle all over town. Is that clear?"

"Of course, Logan," Betty said. "I wouldn't dream of it."

Yeah, you would. He hung up the phone.

"What's gonna become the subject of tittle-tattle?" Lyle asked, wandering back into the room with a slice of cold pizza.

"Nothing." Logan got up and marched past his brother.

He had to talk to Charlotte. Had to find out if she'd taken the test.

That was all he could focus on right now. That and the fact that deep down, past the anxiety and the concern and the frustration was a warm spot in the pit of his belly.

A strange inexplicable warmth that was telling him—against all notions of sense and sanity—that this development didn't necessarily have to be a bad thing.

★

"CHARLOTTE? YOU AWAKE in there?"

Charlie rolled over at the soft tap on the door. She could pretend to be asleep—the lump of anxiety in her stomach still felt like the *Titanic* sinking to the bottom of the ocean. But before she could make up her mind whether to answer Logan's request or not, the door opened.

She scrubbed her eyes, to make sure there was no evidence of the foolish tears, and sat up. "I was just falling asleep," she lied.

"In your clothes?" he said.

Bollocks.

Not waiting for more of an invitation, he walked across the room.

The mattress dipped as he sat down beside her and placed a hand on her thigh. The warmth seeped through her clothing and she felt the *Titanic*-sized lump of anxiety rise out of the churning ocean in her stomach and bob into her throat.

She wanted to lean into his arms, to let him hold her, but she couldn't. She had to be independent, self-contained. She didn't want to be weak and needy. It made her feel like that little girl who had once grabbed her father's trouser leg and begged him to stay home only to be shaken off as if she were an annoying puppy and told by the nanny. *"Stop creating a scene, Charlotte. Your father has important business; he can't stay home to look after you."*

"We need to talk," he said.

"What about?" she said, her voice little more than a whisper—as the well of things she couldn't talk about threatened to gag her.

"First off, I've got to give you some advice," he said, the crinkle of sympathy round his eyes making the tears sting again. "Next time you need to buy something private, don't go into Marietta Pharmacy. Carol Bingley, the manager, is a lady who couldn't keep a secret if her life depended on it."

Oh crap. Oh crap. Oh crap.

The choking sensation in her throat became unbearable. And the dumb, stupid tears leaked out. "You know about the pregnancy test?"

He nodded, then without asking her permission, he folded her shaking body into his arms.

He held her tight as the tears she didn't want to shed ran down her cheeks, and the choking sobs she'd been keeping in for what felt like years welled up in her chest and spilled out.

She clung on to his solid strength as the storm surged. The smell of leather, and horses, and laundry soap and Logan finally settling her, until the choking sobs had turned to whimpering hiccoughs.

She bit into her lip to stop them, his murmured assurances as he stroked her hair both comforting and mortifying.

Finally, finally, she felt strong enough to pull out of his arms. She scrubbed the salty residue off her cheeks. Now she knew why other women carried tissues around with them.

"Have you taken the test yet?" he asked, firm and straightforward.

She shook her head. "The instructions say you should do it first thing in the morning, to get the most accurate result. I don't want to bugger it up." Like she'd buggered up so much else.

She could see all the other questions lurking in his eyes. Why hadn't she told him? How long had she suspected she might be pregnant? What did she plan to do if she was? Why had she just had a crying fit in his arms worthy of The Madwoman of Chaillot?

All questions she did not have coherent answers to anymore. But instead of asking them, he cupped her chin, let his thumb drift over the puffy skin under her eyes and said. "Okay."

Just like that. As if he had her back, regardless of what she did, or didn't do.

She leant into his touch, wanting to take the comfort he offered. Wanting so much to feel secure. To feel loved. If just for a little while.

She sniffed, imagining she must look a total mess. "Sorry I behaved like such a prize bitch downstairs. I've been a bit stressed," she said.

His lips quirked in that lazy seductive smile she adored. "Understandable," he murmured.

His hand dropped to her shoulder, and his thumb caressed her collarbone.

The ripple of awareness, of arousal, felt empowering. Simple and uncomplicated, this was a need for him she understood.

"I don't suppose…" She hesitated. "I don't suppose

you'd consider making love to me?" she asked, hating the plea in her voice and the blood rushing to her already sore cheeks.

She needed this to take the pressure off. They both did.

"The headache's gone?" he asked, the husky tone of voice telling her all she needed to know. He had this.

She smiled. "I guess it must be."

Without saying more, he drew her to him and pressed his lips to hers.

The kiss was tender, seeking, requesting permission instead of demanding it.

She sucked on his tongue, embracing the wave of hunger that swept through her. Desperate not to feel the emotion.

He undressed her, slowly, patiently. Then undressed himself. Joining her on the bed, he teased and tortured her yearning flesh—knowing just how to touch her, to kiss her, to drive her effortlessly to a peak. While she was still floating on the waves of afterglow, she heard the rustle of clothing, the rip of foil, and then he eased inside her.

She tightened around him, another climax rolling over her as if the first one had never ended.

At last they lay in the darkened room, her back wedged against his chest, his arm tight around her midriff, holding her securely. As if he'd never let her go.

He found the quilt and yanked it up to cover them both.

Her eyelids felt unbearably heavy as she watched the fat flakes of fresh snow falling outside the window.

The exhaustion did nothing to halt the renewed wobble

in her stomach as he murmured against her hair. "Go to sleep, Charlotte. I've got you."

This wasn't real, not really. She knew that. It was just a beautiful dream.

Logan Tate had sworn to serve and protect, not just his community as a Deputy Sheriff, and his little brother Lyle during the unhappy years after his mother's death, but also Harry Monroe's legacy and pretty much everyone who had ever come into his life—including her. Because that was the kind of guy he was.

He took responsibility. He did the right thing. He always had your back if you needed him to.

And that's why she hadn't wanted to tell him about the pregnancy test. It seemed so clear now. Because if it said she was having his child, he would convince himself he loved her—would never acknowledge how fickle, how flighty, how undeserving she was of his care and protection.

Tomorrow she would have to deal with that harsh reality, for the both of them.

Her heart stuttered and stirred as his hand stroked her thigh in an absent, possessive caress and his breathing evened out into deep rhythmic sleep.

She snuggled into him and shut out the depressing thoughts.

Tomorrow would be here soon enough. Tonight she was too tired to do anything but relish the feel of his arms around her and let her mind float on all those impossible dreams.

Chapter Thirteen

"ARE YOU SURE you don't want me to stay? The guys can wait. I don't want you to have to do this on your own."

Charlie's heart throbbed in her throat at the conviction in Logan's face as he sat on the bed. She squeezed her thighs together, so desperate to pee she was worried she might wet the bed if he didn't leave soon.

She'd been listening to him shower, and get ready to go into town for the renovation day the calendar dudes had scheduled for Harry's House a week ago—which she couldn't have been more grateful for.

She'd thought it all through. Logan couldn't be here. She had to do the test on her own. And then decide how to handle it. She'd made a ninny of herself last night. Made him feel responsible when he wasn't. She wasn't going to be that weak and pathetic again.

Unfortunately she hadn't factored in her weak bladder, or Logan's complete inability to take a hint.

"Honestly, Logan, I'd *rather* do this on my own," she said, deciding to be blunt, before she ended up in a pool of her own making.

"You sure."

"Yes, I'm sure. I'll text you the result. If it's…" She swallowed, not sure she could even say it. "If it's something we need to discuss, we can talk about it tonight."

He didn't look too happy about her decision.

"Okay, I guess if that's the way you want to play it."

"It is."

Nodding, he got off the bed. Leaning down, he kissed her on the lips, the lingering taste of him crucifying her almost as much as her bursting bladder. But when he straightened, he didn't leave. He stood for two pregnant seconds before saying. "Whatever the result, I want you to know I'd be happy, Charlotte. Because you make me happy."

What?

It was the last thing she had expected him to say. "I…" she began, then her tongue just stalled. What did he mean by that?

"Don't freak out," he said, his lips crinkling with humor. "All I'm saying is. I like having you here." He thrust his hands through his hair, frustrated, searching for the right words. "I like having you here a lot. I think we're great together. And I want you to stay. Not just for a few weeks but for…you know…for longer. With me. If you want to. And I hope you do."

"But I can't stay," she murmured, horrified by the foolish spurt of hope blossoming in her chest at the warmth in his voice. Was he saying what she thought he was saying? That he loved her?

"I don't know what to say," she added.

Which had to be a first for her.

"Then don't say anything, Charlotte. I'm just asking you to think about it, okay. I know it's a lot to ask. And it's kind of sudden. And I should have told you this before now. But I just don't want you to panic if the result is positive. Can you do that for me?"

She nodded, although she was already panicking.

"Great." He kissed her again. "I'll be back at four, no later. Text me—whatever the news is I want to know."

She nodded again, in a daze as he left.

How could he sound eager, excited even? When all she felt was sick with guilt and anxiety?

She climbed out of bed as she heard the door shut downstairs. Wiping the steam off the window, she watched him trudge through the new layer of snow.

He waved as he got into the truck. She waved back.

Her hand hung suspended in midair as the truck disappeared from view round the side of the stables—the urge to pee like a racehorse having disappeared with it.

✪

NEGATIVE. NADA. NO *blue line. You're not pregnant with Logan Tate's baby.*

Charlie dumped the testing stick in the trash and washed

her hands.

Her still-shaking hands.

Why didn't she feel relieved? Pleased? Overjoyed? The problem was solved. This was good news.

Except it wasn't, because all she felt was numb and hollow and terrified. Exactly the same way she'd felt before peeing on the bloody stick and waiting the required two minutes to get the result.

She sat back down on the toilet seat, trying to make sense of her reaction. As the *Titanic*-sized lump sunk back to the bottom of her stomach. She finally faced the truth. The pregnancy scare had been a distraction, or rather an abstraction. Just another way to avoid the feelings that she had been shoving to one side and refusing to acknowledge now for days, maybe even weeks.

The feelings Logan had had the guts to voice and she hadn't. Because Logan was brave and strong and bold… And she was a coward.

She'd only gone and fallen in love with the man.

She sunk her head into her hands, frustration and fear and confusion overwhelming her—and she wanted to cry some more. But she'd done all her crying yesterday and it hadn't solved anything; if anything it had made the problem worse.

She couldn't do this. Logan would be back at four and he'd want an answer. Baby or no baby he would want to know—what she thought of him? Of them? Of the suggestion that she stay at the Double T? And attempt to build a life here?

And while a part of her wanted so much to say yes. Let's go for it. Let's try. I love you. I love this country, this town—even after only three weeks it feels special. You feel special. Maybe one day we could even have babies together.

A much bigger part of her—the scared little girl inside her—was simply terrified that she would make that commitment to him and then muck it up.

I can't stay.

Standing, she grabbed her toiletry bag and swept everything inside. She raced into the other room, and located her pack in the bottom of the closet where she'd left it the day she'd arrived at the ranch.

She shoved her clothes inside, then dragged the pack into Logan's room, the room they'd shared. She shoved everything of hers in the room into her pack too, while trying not to look at the bed. Or the Deputy's badge he'd left on the dresser.

It took her a frantic half an hour to get everything packed. At which point she stopped running around long enough to have another problem slam into her.

The project. Oh shit.

She made a frantic phone call to McKenna Sheenan at Big Sky Photography and thanked God when the woman agreed to do Jonah Clark's shoot, if the guy every replied to any texts. Then she called Ally Clark, Jonah's sister-in-law, an event planner who had offered to help out with the scheduling and the hunt for a designer who would work for free if Charlie needed it weeks ago. Ally was surprisingly amenable, although obviously a bit surprised at the sudden rush. Charlie put together an email to her, attaching all the files of the shots she'd taken and detailing all the links and passwords to the calendar project's social media properties.

But the hollow feeling became a yawning chasm in her stomach as she pressed send.

This was for the best. This was the way it was always supposed to be.

By ten o'clock she had everything done. Her life at the Double T, her involvement with the project—it had all been erased. She'd even managed to dismantle the darkroom and pack it into boxes, ready for McKenna to come over and pick up the next day. She stuffed the black-and-white prints of Logan into her pack, just as Lyle appeared at the front door, returning from the stock check he'd been saddled with that morning.

"Lyle, I need a lift," she said, adrenaline and panic charging through her system.

"Sure thing, sugar," he said. "I'm heading in to help out with the house renovation. Logan texted me to ask me to nag you about something or other. So this is good. You can talk to him direct."

Her heart lurched. The guilt and grief all but crippling her. She'd texted Logan to tell him the test was negative two hours ago, then turned off her phone.

"No, no, I need a lift to the bus station. I've got to head out of town. I've… I've been offered an important new commission."

Lyle frowned, noticing the bulging pack and boxes of darkroom equipment she had stacked next to the door.

"Hold on a minute. You're leaving? When are you coming back?"

"I'm not. The project's done. Or almost done. I've handed over the reins and all the shots to Ally Clark, and McKenna's going to handle Jonah's shoot when he finally stops behaving like a pill."

Lyle's face hardened, the dancing light in his eyes she had become so used to disappearing. "What about Logan?"

"What *about* Logan?" she said, struggling to sound nonchalant.

He stared at her for the longest time. "You're not even going to tell him?" he said. But there was no surprise in his voice—only the bite of cynicism. And, not for the first time, it occurred to her there was much more to Lyle Tate than the reckless flirt he pretended to be.

"I'll give him a call when I get a chance," she said, even though she knew she wouldn't.

It would be too painful. Too hard for them both. Logan wouldn't understand. Because he was strong and brave and dependable. He did everything straight and above board. He didn't have doubts or anxieties. He was selfless, not selfish.

Unlike her.

And he would never run away from a problem. The way she had been doing her whole life. Which was exactly why it would be better for them both if she left.

Lyle shouldered her pack and held open the door. "There's a bus to Livingston at a quarter to eleven."

He hadn't asked where she was headed. But she didn't correct him. Because they both knew she didn't have an important commission.

Her heart imploded as she stepped off the old porch. She listened to her feet crunch in the snow as she followed Lyle to his truck and climbed into the cab.

They didn't talk during the drive into town. Because really, what else was there left to say?

Chapter Fourteen

LOGAN YANKED DOWN his mask and threw another length of drywall on the pile of debris he'd been accumulating all morning, the uneasy feeling that had been riding him downgraded a notch when he saw his brother appear in the doorway.

"About damn time," he said. "Where the hell have you been?"

Demolishing the stud partition was dusty, backbreaking work, and it had gone some way to curbing Logan's frustration with Charlotte, but not nearly enough.

Why the heck hadn't she answered any of his texts? He'd gotten one curt message to say the pregnancy test was negative—which had left him feeling more ambivalent than relieved—and then nothing. Not a damn word. And all his calls had gone to voice mail. It was now eleven o'clock and he hadn't heard from her since eight. He kept telling himself to calm down and keep his mind on the construction work. She was probably just in her darkroom, or stooped over her laptop, busy playing around with her photos in Photoshop, or on the phone organizing some deal or other to do with the project.

But something didn't feel right. And after last night's crying jag and the stunned look in Charlotte's eyes when he'd laid his feelings bare this morning, he wasn't convinced the radio silence was a good sign.

Most of the other First Responders who had come together to fundraise with the calendar were dotted through the old timber-framed building—all of them much more comfortable pitching in with the renovations than taking their shirts off for charity. When Logan had arrived at eight, Kyle Cavasos had been taking point—because he had a knack for this stuff—and the fireman had directed him in here to show him how to saw through and then rip out the stud wall they no longer needed.

But ripping down drywall had stopped being able to cure Logan's uneasiness hours ago.

"I had to do the stock check this morning, remember?" Lyle answered as he picked his way toward Logan through the debris. "That's where I've been, so back the hell off."

Logan's uneasiness shot straight into the danger zone at the surly response. His brother looked pissed—which wasn't like Lyle at all; he was usually a pretty sunny guy, even when he had to devote his day off to manual labor.

And Lyle had been due to join them over an hour ago—no way should riding out to check the pregnant cows in the calving fields have taken this long.

"Why didn't you answer my text about Charlotte?" he

persisted—the uneasy feeling now tying his guts into greasy knots.

His brother's frown became more pronounced. "I'm not your messenger. You got something to say to her, you need to contact her yourself."

The evasive answer had alarm bells ringing in Logan's head—the greasy knots turning to burning asteroids in the pit of his stomach. His brother knew something. Something he wasn't saying.

"What the fuck is going on?" Logan grabbed the front of Lyle's shirt and yanked him close. "Something's wrong. I know it."

"Leave me alone." Lyle struggled out of his grip, his face turning red with fury. "She left, okay. She left you. And she's not coming back," he shouted, the words hitting Logan like blows. "I told you she wouldn't stick, but you didn't listen."

"She... What?" Logan choked on the word, the shock reverberating through him, making his knees feel like rubber.

Why would she do that? After last night? After the past month? After everything he'd said to her this morning? How could she just leave? When she knew how he felt about her? When he was pretty sure she felt the same way about him?

"I'm sorry, man," Lyle murmured. The spurt of temper had been replaced with bone-deep regret as his brother placed his hand on Logan's shoulder. "I should never have brought her out to the ranch. I just didn't think you'd fall for her..." His brother looked devastated. As if this was somehow his fault. "I screwed up. Like I'm always screwing up," he added. "I'm sorry."

What the hell was his brother apologizing for? Charlotte coming to the ranch had been the best thing to happen to Logan for as long as he could remember. How could his brother not know that?

Logan shook off the confusing thoughts.

He didn't have time to process Lyle's weird apology right now. He had to stay focused, work this out, deal with one thing at a time. And the thing he needed to deal with first was getting Charlotte back.

He'd scared her off, with his declaration that morning. He'd known she would probably freak out, but he'd gone ahead and said it anyway—before leaving her alone to do the pregnancy test. So now he had to handle the fallout from those dumb decisions.

"Where did she go?" he asked.

Lyle's eyebrows rose. "You're not seriously going after her? She just gave you the kiss-off? Haven't you got any pride?"

"So help me, Lyle, if you don't cut the bullshit and tell me where she went in the next two seconds…" Logan's voice rose to a roar in direct correlation with his temper—he did not have time for this. "I am going to punch you through what's left of that goddamn wall."

"Jesus, man. Chill the hell out." Lyle raised his hands in a defensive gesture, staring at Logan as if he'd just sprouted an extra head. "She got the bus to Livingston. It left about ten minutes ago."

"Here, take these." Tearing off his workman's gloves, Logan slapped them against Lyle's chest. "Finish the wall."

"Where are you going?" Lyle asked as he scooped up the gloves.

"I'm going to get her back," he yelled over his shoulder as he charged through the house and shot out the front door.

He ran to his truck and climbed in, then drove like a bat out of hell down 2nd and onto Main Street.

This wasn't happening, not again. Not if he could help it.

His mom had died on him and he hadn't been able to do a thing about it, because he'd been a terrified little kid.

Then his father had grieved himself to death—and Logan hadn't done a damn thing about that either, because he'd been more scared of people finding out his old man was a mean drunk than he was in getting the guy help.

And Harry had died too, because instead of stopping to help his friend fix the tire on the side of the road that night, Logan had driven on by to get back to his cozy living room, a hot meal, and some dumb football game.

But the buck stopped with Charlotte.

No way was he losing her, or letting her throw away everything they could have together. Everything they could build. Not until he had done every single thing in his power to stop her.

With that in mind, he hung a left at Our Lady of the Angels on Main Street then a right on Front and screeched to a halt outside the Sheriff's Office. He could see Betty staring out the window, her eyes as big as saucers as he jumped into one of the cars, leant under the dash to deal with the ignition, and peeled out of the lot.

He expected news of him hot-wiring his own squad car was going to be all over town in about five seconds, but he didn't give a damn.

He needed more authority than his battered truck if he was going to stop a bus.

★

CHARLIE FELT SICK. Sick and drained and so hollow inside her stomach felt as if it had been sucked into a black hole. But she had done the right thing.

A clean break was best, for Logan as well as her. What was the point of pretending they could make a life together when they couldn't?

Even so it hurt to watch the snowy ridges of Copper Mountain, and the Ponderosa forest roll away as the bus lumbered its way toward Livingston.

She swallowed heavily. They would be passing the place where she and Logan had met in a minute. The land looked different now, starkly white with its coating of snow, but still so breathtaking.

Her heart cracked, rent down the middle by her own cowardice. But just as the bus came round the turn, a police car's siren cut through the sound of people chatting and the bus's laboring engine. The driver braked and everyone shunted forward, before the bus shuddered to a stop at the roadside.

Charlie grasped the seat back in front of her, and stood up—trying to see past the heads of other curious passengers as the driver opened the door. A blast of cold air reached all the way to Charlie's spot near the back.

A man appeared in shirt sleeves and dusty jeans, his dark hair disheveled, his face grim. And then his blue eyes locked on to her face.

Charlie's heart galloped full tilt into her throat.

Logan? Logan was on the bus. And now Logan was stalking toward her.

She blinked several times, trying to clamp down on the whisper of hope whistling through her hollow stomach like a spring wind thawing winter snow.

He stopped in front of her, looking mighty solid for a figment of her imagination. "Where's your luggage?"

"It's in the hold," she managed round the feeling of unreality.

This could not actually be happening. She was dreaming this.

No way would Logan Tate, law-abiding Sheriff's Deputy, have just stopped a bus on the highway in his squad car for no reason.

He reached up into the rack above her head and got her coat and camera bag, then gripped her arm and tugged her into the aisle. "Come on, this is your stop."

"It's...what?" she said, but he was already escorting her down the aisle—past the shocked expressions of the ten other passengers who were all staring at her as if she were an escaped convict who had just been caught.

"Leave her luggage at the next stop," he told the driver. "We'll pick it up tomorrow."

"Yes sir, Deputy Tate," the driver said.

Wait a fricking minute, he's not even on duty. Can't you see he's not wearing his bloody badge?

She screamed the thought in her head, but she was still too stunned to make her tongue work.

And before she could get her wits about her enough to shout the words to the driver for real, she had been bundled down the steps of the vehicle and was standing on the side of the road with a madman, shivering, while the bus disappeared in the distance.

Logan wrapped the coat round her shoulders. "Put it on," he said, as if he hadn't just lost his mind. "It's freezing out here."

She stuffed her arms into the sleeves, while he bent to slip the buttons into their holes. She couldn't stop shaking—the sight of him, the scent of him, so wonderful and yet so terrifying.

"Logan, what are you doing here?" she said, through her chattering teeth—the weird sensation of wanting to laugh and weep at exactly the same time tearing her to pieces inside.

Why had he done this? Did he want to torture them both with a protracted goodbye?

"What am *I* doing here?" he shouted back, the frustration emanating off him in waves. "What the hell are *you* doing here, Charlotte? Running off without a goddamn word?"

Guilt assailed her. "You didn't get my text?"

"Of course I got your text. At eight a.m. And I've been trying to contact you ever since. And then Lyle shows up at Harry's House to tell me you've left on the bus and you're not coming back. Are you nuts? Why the hell would you do that?"

She wrapped her arms around her midriff, the accusation, the anger, but most of all the stunned hurt in his tone like a knife in her gut. "I couldn't stay. I just couldn't. I had to go."

"Why couldn't you stay? Why did you have to go? I want answers, Charlotte, not platitudes."

She bit into her lip, looked away from him, the stinging tears threatening to turn what was already a bad melodrama into a total catastrophe.

How had it come to this? Did he really want her to spell it out for him? All the reasons why she was so wrong for him? List all her bloody faults and inadequacies.

"You want to know what I think?" he said.

She shook her head. She didn't want to know what he thought.

He touched her cheek with chilly fingers, and forced her face round to his.

"I think you're scared."

"Of course I'm scared," she spluttered. "I'm bloody terrified. I don't want to feel like this. I don't want to love you. And I don't want you to love me. Because I'll muck it all up and then we'll both be miserable."

A slow smile curved his lips. "Why would you muck it up?"

Why was he smiling? Hadn't he heard what she'd said?

Her frustration spiked, her temper burning through at least some of the fear.

"Because that's what I do, Logan. Haven't you figured it out yet? I don't stick. I don't settle. I don't have relationships." Her teeth started chattering again, but it wasn't from the cold this time, it was from the earthquake of emotion pouring through her body. "I meet guys. Sometimes I screw them. And then I move on." He was still smiling at her. Had he gone deaf as well as blind? "You don't understand that because you're not like that. You're brave, and bold and strong and true—inside and out. And you've never run away from anything in your whole life."

Instead of saying anything, he simply grasped her shoul-

HEIDI RICE

ders and dragged her into his body. Pressing his lips against her hair, he banded his arms around her.

She stiffened in his arms. She couldn't take the comfort he offered. Not again. She didn't deserve it. But then he began to talk against her hair, as his hands rubbed her back.

"A while back you told me you wished you could brand my pop for what he did to me. Do you remember that?"

She nodded, the unshed tears making her throat hurt at the memory of that beautiful day.

"Well, right about now," he continued, "I wish I could drop-kick your dumb, useless parents into the middle of next week for you."

She jerked back. "Why?"

"Because they made you think you're not worth anything. And you are, Charlotte. You're worth so much. You're worth everything to me."

"But how can you think that, when I'm such a coward?"

He touched a finger to her lips to stop the flow of words, of recriminations.

"You think I'm not scared too?" he said. "I am. I'm terrified. I know what it's like to love someone and then lose them. I thought I could anesthetize myself from ever having to feel that pain again by holing myself up at the Double T and never looking for anything more. But then you came along with your smart mouth and your sexy moves and your compassion and determination. And you made me see that what I had wasn't living, it was existing. You made me want more, Charlotte, so much more. And that more is you." He cupped her face in his hands, all the love he felt for her plain on his face. Her teeth stopped chattering, the warmth suffusing her whole body, like lava flowing from a volcano that had been dormant for far too long.

"I'm still scared though," she said.

"Me too," he said. "So what? You really want to miss out on all the good stuff we could have just because you're scared?"

"But, Logan, what about the future? I completely freaked out over the pregnancy test. And you said you'd be happy either way. You're the sort of guy who will want to have children, a family. What if I'm never ready to do that?"

"Charlotte, we've been together four weeks. I'll probably want to have kids one day. I guess. I'd love to see you all fat and round with my baby in your belly," he teased.

"But…" she began.

"Hush now," he murmured. "But what I want more is to see the Double T become what it was always meant to be. What it was before my mom passed. I want to see it become a home again."

The wistful tone made her heart ache.

"It would be a great place to bring up kids…" he added. "But if you're sure that's not what you want. I can reconsider. Are you sure you don't want to have kids? Ever?"

He'd turned the tables on her. And she didn't have an answer. Because with Logan, everything was different.

Hadn't a part of her almost been disappointed when the stick had stayed negative? Not because she wanted to get accidentally pregnant after four weeks with him—but because the idea of having children with Logan felt…well, possible.

"No I'm not," she answered. "I'm not sure of anything anymore." *Except how much I love you.*

"Then what are we arguing about?"

"I don't know," she said, the smile slow and a little painful, but there nonetheless.

Cupping her shoulders he looked into her face, his own smile both sexy and sure. "Then how about we go home now? Because I'm about to freeze my nuts off. And I've still got to explain to Sheriff Walton why I stole my own squad car."

She chuckled.

Home. It was such a simple word. But one she'd never fully understood until this moment when she felt for the first time as if she had somewhere to belong.

"Yes, please," she said.

He whooped, lifting her off her feet and swinging her around.

She laughed, his joy infectious, as he planted her back on her feet.

He clasped her face in cold hands and covered her mouth with his. His tongue was hot and avid, and demanding, his body strong and true and hers. All hers, as she kissed him back with all the happiness and hunger in her heart, the peaks of Copper Mountain shadowing the snowy landscape, and watching over them like a benevolent giant.

What were you thinking, you ninny? You're not going to mess this up. Not now you've finally found a home… In Logan Tate's arms.

The End

The Men of Marietta Series

When there isn't enough money to make Harry's House a functional afterschool center, the Montana First Responders decide they need to step up, and really turn up the heat. The Men of Marietta Calendar is created with pages filled of sexy guys willing to do just about anything for a great cause....

Book 1: *Tempting the Deputy* by Heidi Rice

Book 2: *Flirting with Fire* by Kate Hardy

Book 3: *Daring the Pilot* by Jeannie Moon

Book 4: *Falling for the Ranger* by Kaylie Newell

Book 5: *Burning with Desire* by Patricia W. Fischer

Available now at your favorite online retailer!

More by Heidi Rice

Tempting the Knight

Book 1 in the Fairy Tales of New York series

Sleepless in London

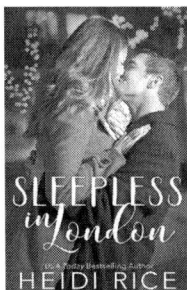

Available now at your favorite online retailer!

About the Author

USA Today Bestselling and RITA-nominated author Heidi Rice is married with two sons (which gives her rather too much of an insight into the male psyche). She also works as a film journalist and was born in Notting Hill in West London (before it became as chi-chi as it is in the film starring Hugh Grant). She now lives in Islington in North London – a stone's throw away from where they shot Four Weddings and a Funeral... (She has asked Hugh to stop stalking her, but will he listen?!)

She loves her job because it involves sitting down at her computer each day and getting swept up in a world of high emotions, sensual excitement, funny feisty women, sexy tortured men and glamorous locations where laundry doesn't exist ... Not bad, eh.

Visit her website Heidi-Rice.com

Thank you for reading

Tempting the Deputy

If you enjoyed this book, you can find more from all our great authors at TulePublishing.com, or from your favorite online retailer.

TULE
PUBLISHING

Printed in Great Britain
by Amazon